THIS IS
GOD'S
COUNTRY

THIS IS GOD'S COUNTRY

a novel

by

BRUCE K BECK

AUDACITY BOOKS

WE DARE TO TELL THE TRUTH

New York

This book is dedicated to
Patricia Wynne and Maceo Mitchell,
for their example.

<u>*Chapter One*</u>

It was early on a Monday morning that spring in 1990 when the phone rang. I had no intention of picking up until I heard a familiar voice on the answering machine:

"Kit, it's your mother. I hate to have to tell you this, but your daddy is dying."

I dashed for the phone. Really, how could I not? "Momma, Daddy's been dying ever since I was twenty. What makes today different?"

"Kit, you can talk as cold as you want, but I know you love your daddy."

She always did know how to exasperate me. "Momma, please tell me what's going on."

"He wants to see you. You'd better come soon. This week."

"But, Momma, I'm so busy at work right now. And Gabriel has a show opening in two weeks. I can't leave him now."

"He wants to see you both."

"He wants what?"

"He wants to see you and Gabriel both."

"Momma, I . . . I don't know what to say. Let me call you back this evening. I'll talk to Gabriel. Maybe we can figure something out. Don't count on it! But I'll try. Anyway, let me go. I'll call you after seven. Is that okay?"

"Kit, I know you'll do the right thing," Momma said.

She should have been a harpist, the way she can pluck each string. Instead of a harpy, I thought. No, that wasn't fair. Momma was always as fair as she could manage to be. But when it came to a choice between her husband and her son, well, I wasn't exactly thrown under the bus. And yet?

"Gabriel, you won't believe who just called."

"You're being mysterious," Gabriel said.

"Sorry. That was Momma. She says Daddy's dying. I know, what else is new? But she says this time it's serious. He wants to see us."

"He wants to see *us*?" my beautiful mate responded.

"Momma said, 'Your daddy wants to see you and Gabriel both,'"

"Kitten, I can't deal with this right now. Could we talk about it tonight?"

"Of course," I said. "I know you want to stay at the studio as long as possible. I'll bring something with me after work. How about a falafel plate? From Mahmoud's?"

"With extra hot sauce?"

"Of course. You have some wine there, yes?"

"There's plenty left from the case you ordered last week. Not to worry," Gabriel said. "Let me go, Kitten. I feel really pressured to finish."

"Of course you do, Angel," I said. "You tackle that Muse and don't let her up until the new canvas is finished. But save the victory dance for me. I want it all. Always did."

"You're the only Muse I've ever needed. And I save *everything* for you."

"See that you do!" I said. "On your way, young man!" And he was out the door. We were not really *all that* young anymore. But forty felt perfect to me. Like a gift. Like a chance at adulthood without the wrinkles. I felt really buoyant. Maybe for the first time in my life. Not only did Gabriel still love me after twenty years, but I loved him even more than I had been able to, I think, in the early years.

I pulled myself together and headed off to work. Never once, in the last eighteen years, had I dreaded going to work. The Metropolitan Museum of Art is such a glorious place to be that even if the atmosphere in the backstage curatorial offices had been creepy—which it most certainly was not—I could have been content just to be in that building every day.

I had no illusions about my brilliance in the field of art history. But I had managed to complete a degree in a credible university program, and the fact that my family connections were good did no harm. Even though Daddy had more-or-less disowned me— more about that later. Institutions like the Met were famous for hiring promising youngsters who could be underpaid because, presumably, they had family resources to cushion them.

I always said I didn't have that cushion, but the Christmas and birthday checks from Momma went a long way toward keeping Gabriel and me in house and home—while Gabe, too, developed his career. Almost in spite of myself, I developed a—slight—expertise in the works of John Singer Sargent and his contemporaries. I don't envy the social mores of the Late Victorians and Edwardians, but I fell in love with Sargent's vision.

Delicious brushwork, yes. Perfect pitch with portraiture—grand, and yet heartbreakingly human. Could he flatter? Absolutely. Are the subjects also real? Stunningly so. Given a choice between a Sargent and a photo, perhaps we all might decide to see the photograph first. And then most of us will opt for the Sargent, I think, not just because it's prettier—often—but because it tells the truth.

The small canvases and the watercolors leave me speechless, and the male nudes are so stunning that perhaps the only regret of my entire life was that I didn't own one. And don't get me started on Sargent's anti-war paintings. That panoramic depiction of gassed soldiers in WWI—one of Sargent's largest canvases—is like an assault on the heart. That he was able to drop all pretense of prettiness and civility to point out the monstrosity of the damage and loss from that fruitless war is so moving that . . . well, I told you not to get me started.

I got through my workday, stopped for a swim at the Y, and headed downtown.

"Gabriel, this is just glorious," I said, as I unpacked our supper at the studio. The canvas he was finishing was large, about 6' X 9'. It was beautifully drafted and yet filled with luscious splashes of color, almost primary color by the look of it, but always mixed with consummate skill. Gabriel's brushwork looked both random and perfectly controlled, at the same time. I thought it was his best work ever.

"Thank you, Kitten," Gabriel said. "I love it, too. Now, what's this about your family?" he asked amid bites of falafel and hummus and salad.

"Momma says Daddy wants to see us. Yes, *us*. I know the timing couldn't be worse for you, but I was thinking: I can probably get a week or so off. There's nothing crucial going on at the Met just now. If we fly down day-after-tomorrow, I bet I can get you home the next day—two days tops. I think I can't avoid this, and I want you with me if at all possible. But only if you feel you can spare two days or so. It's your call."

"I wouldn't leave New York right now for any other reason," Gabriel said, "but if you feel it's important, then let's do it. I'll finish this canvas tomorrow and set up the last one. And then, it'll be fine."

That's how it happened, that spring Monday in 1990, that we decided to return to our hometown together for the first time in twenty years. But the whole thing won't make any sense to anyone unless I start at the beginning.

When I was born, in the winter of 1950, my parents named me Christopher Bullard Prescott. Christopher was Daddy's favorite uncle, and Momma was proud to be a Bullard. There had been Bullards in the county since before the Revolution. So she passed the name to me. Claysville is in Prescott County, so you know Daddy was proud of that. Like most of the family stuff, it left me rather cold. But like so much else, it made life easier. And so I accepted it without too much thought. Some Southern families were big on Junior, II, III, and IV. The Prescotts considered that *arriviste*. They preferred to individualize.

Apparently I was a difficult delivery, because Momma's doctor warned her not to attempt another pregnancy: it might kill her. So that's how I came to be the only child. I think they had planned on several more kids, but it wasn't to be. According to family history, I was called Kit by our housekeeper, Esther Graves. Supposedly she looked down on baby me in my bassinet and said, "Why, he's just as pretty as a little kit fox." I never trusted family lore too much, but this one is probably true. Esther had a perfect right to call me whatever she liked, considering it would be her job to raise me—with financial support from Daddy, of course, but with not all that much input from him or Momma otherwise. And I've always thought it a tribute to Esther's wisdom that I managed to turn out as well as I did.

By the time I was five I had heard the story a hundred times of how Daddy had come to build our house. It seems he had bought about five acres just west of downtown. From the Clay family (think Claysville). They owned a huge wooded property surrounding a small lake—Clay's Lake, of course. But the year before I was born, the Clays sold off some residential parcels—to good families, of course. And just when Daddy was deciding which architect he wanted to build his new house, he had a business run-in with Mr. Clay. Something about property Daddy owned that Clay needed for a textile mill.

When the business situation turned ugly, Daddy sold the plot of land on Clay's Lake to the man who owned the Chevrolet dealership in Claysville. Chevys driving on the little lane that encircled the lake—the same lane that Mrs. Clay drove in her Mercedes--that was what Daddy wanted. And he got it. And he made money on the deal. And so he decided to build on an even bigger piece of land he already owned. It was farther west. Just on the edge of the Country Club. Daddy would have preferred to be a little closer to town, but he settled for a beautiful ten-acre plot where he could plan the biggest house in Claysville. Was it? Maybe. Daddy wanted it to be.

I didn't share much with my parents. Particularly not anything to do with my feelings. They had never expressed all that much interest in anything to do with me except how I made them look. Or at least that's how it seemed to me at the time. So I kept my own counsel but played the game. School work seemed easy, so I got good grades without much effort. I drew the line at sports, though. All the ball games seemed exceptionally stupid to me—a colossal waste of time. But I did learn tennis, for the sake of form. And I was reasonably good at it, though it provided no real pleasure. What I did enjoy was swimming. It suited me, so I pursued it enough to get rather good. Nothing Olympic, mind you. Just competence and speed. And it kept my body toned, as well. And that made me happy.

There was another baby boy born the same day as I was, but on the other side of town. Gabriel Elijah Williamson had the good fortune to be born into a family with a whole lot of love. I envied that in later years. But his parents had very little money, and Gabriel would have to face the unenviable task of being a black boy growing up in the South. Through a complex convergence of circumstances and luck, he survived it.

In those days, I always thought, ugly black children were maybe more likely to be ignored by white people, and therefore safer. Whereas pretty black children inspired a complex reaction that surely involved both jealousy and lust.   Not a nice combination. And Gabriel was exceptionally pretty. Still is. He could use his beauty to charm all the matriarchal women around him, and they, in turn, taught him how to stay out of Whitey's way. For the most part. And because Gabriel was also sharp as a whip and talented, it worked.

Gabriel and I never met in Claysville while we were growing up. If he had been Esther's nephew— which he was not—then he might have come by the house to help with something-or-other. Otherwise, East and West didn't mingle much. We didn't meet until we both went off to college. It wasn't that I came from a solidly collegiate family. Momma went to Sweet Briar for a year or two. Daddy had a diploma from Davidson. I'm sure I saw it. I think it was genuine. But even though education was not a high priority, I always knew—from birth, without being told—that I was destined for college.

Gabriel's journey was different. The women in his family prized education above everything except faith. The men prized hard work—and family, of course. Family really came first for all of them. From birth Gabriel was groomed for achievement and success. He became a voracious reader. His maternal grandmother was his first teacher. She was followed by a series of dedicated women who got their job done against tough odds. Not everyone—even in Gabriel's own family—encouraged dreams where decent jobs seemed more important. And the Claysville first families had limited interest in encouraging the dark children on the east side of town.

Even the circumstances of our college admissions were telling: I decided on UNC because it was good enough, and because it did not require any particular effort or originality. Gabriel chose it because he could—because he could get in with a full scholarship and then access all the resources of an important Southern university. I went to enjoy myself and try to learn something at the same time, while Gabriel went to bloom. And we both got what we wanted. Plus a lot more.

Chapter Two

The first time I set eyes on Gabriel was in September of our junior year. I took a shortcut to my little apartment one afternoon. It took me past the tennis courts. Tennis doesn't interest me all that much, as I told you, but one of the players certainly did—the slim young man whose creamy brown skin was set off so beautifully by his tennis whites. I couldn't tell you how his opponent looked. Fit young white guys in tennis gear are usually hot as Hell. But I only had eyes for Gabriel.

I watched until Gabriel took the match, and then the two of them shook hands and parted. And then I walked up while Gabe was blotting the sweat from his face and neck. "Good form!" I said. And I meant it.

"Thanks," he said.

"Kit Prescott," I said as I extended my hand.

"Gabriel Williamson," he said as his right hand enclosed mine.

"Do you have time for a beer, or something?" I asked. Eighteen was the legal age for beer and wine in those days in North Carolina, so there were plenty of bars in Chapel Hill near campus.

"Not just now," he said. "I have a lecture at 3:00 I can't miss. Maybe tonight? Around 7:00?"

"7:00 it is. Here's my phone number. Call me. Maybe Pete's Tavern? Or wherever you like."

"Pete's is good. At 7:00, then." We shook hands again, and then I floated home to my place and took a nap. Was I nervous about meeting Gabriel that evening for a beer? Yes! And it wasn't for lack of opportunity. I had hot guys hitting on me all the time, if I do say so myself. It was just that Gabriel was the most glorious male package I ever encountered.

Pete's was not glamorous, but the beer was cold and cheap and available. I showed up a little early. Gabriel arrived on time. We shook hands, again; he joined me at the bar and we ordered some brews.

"Where are you from?" I asked. Getting-to-know-you-speak is always dreary.

"From the next county," he said.

"East or west?" I asked.

"Does it matter?" he asked.

"Not to me," I said.

"I'm from Claysville," he said.

"Shit!" I said. "You're not!"

"You're not from Claysville, too, are you?" he asked.

"Not that I'm particularly proud of it, but yes."

"You said Kit Prescott? As in Prescott County?"

"Guilty."

"Jesus, I'm sharing a Bud with the First Family?"

"We don't get to choose our parents," I said

"No. That's true. It's just that I wasn't expecting it. I go back to Claysville for holidays and every summer to work. But somehow I thought I'd left it behind."

"It doesn't seem to work that way, does it? I've been trying to get away for the last two years, and yet I still feel sucked back into it. Maybe we could make our great escape together!" I couldn't believe I said that, but I did.

"Maybe," Gabriel said. We finished our beers and ordered another round. We exchanged a few pleasantries about campus life, and then I asked:

"Will you come back to my apartment? It's not much, but it's very near. And it's private. No roommates right now."

"Kit, I'd like to. I'd love to, actually, but I have a really early morning. Maybe one day next week?"

"Of course," I said. "You have my number. Choose an evening."

"I will. As soon as I get back to the dorm and check my schedule," he said.

"Gabriel, I have a confession. I don't much like tennis. I just liked watching you."

"Kit, I have a confession as well. I don't really love tennis either. I just like that I can play it well, and that I can beat hot white boys."

"That's reason enough to take up a sport, I think. But what do you love?" I asked.

"I love painting."

"And I love paintings. Interesting confluence of interests," I said. "And attractions."

"What else do you love?" Gabriel asked.

"I swim. It's the only physical activity that's ever really interested me. And when I'm doing laps, I feel like I'm actually part of the universe. The rest of the time, not so much."

"I'd like to see that," Gabe said. "I'd like to see you swimming laps. Or whatever makes you happy."

"There's a meet next week. I'm competing in the butterfly breaststroke and in a relay. You could come."

"I'd like that," he said.

"Really? You'd show up?"

"I always show up."

"It's Wednesday at noon, I think," I said. "You know where the big pool is?"

"Wednesday is my lightest class day. I'm sure it'll be fine."

We finished our brews and headed out into the night. My place was nearby. There was a dark corner just to the side of the entrance to my building. I had lost all interest in handshakes by that point. I pulled Gabriel into the shadows, embraced him, and kissed him. He kissed me back. I embraced him even more firmly and kissed him more deeply. And he responded in kind. When I had caught my breath, I asked, "Gabriel, could we be . . . friends?"

"We could be a lot more than that, if you want it," he said.

"Am I on probation?" I asked.

"Because?"

"Because I'm a Prescott, from fucking Prescott County," I answered.

"I never judge a man by his county," Gabriel said. "Show me your heart. Next time. I want to see it. And all the rest of you, too. All of it. And I'll show you all of me. If you want to see it. And then we'll take it from there." Another kiss, and the moment was over. And he was on his way home.

Young people have physical encounters frequently—some of them very nice, some of them dreary, some of them scary. And some of them dangerous. I can't say I was experienced, but I thought I'd been around the block a couple of times. I learned later that I hadn't even been around the corner yet. But as I made my dazed way up to my little room, I said to myself, *That's it. That's home. That man's embrace and his kiss, that's where I want to spend the rest of my life.*

📖

Gabriel did show up for the swim meet the next Wednesday. He spoke to me before it started. "Good luck!" he said, "or break a flipper? I don't know the proper etiquette."

" 'Good luck' is fine," I said.

"If you can swim as well as you can fill out your Speedos, then you won't need any other advantage," Gabriel said.

"If you keep talking to me that way, I'll be disqualified," I said.

"Then I'll go obediently to the bleachers."

"Yes, please," I said.

We did well. The team from Duke was fiercely competitive, but we took the relay—and it was the timing of my laps that made the difference. I came in second in the breaststroke. I would have been content with second place if Gabriel hadn't been watching. I wanted to win, just so he could be proud of me, really. I didn't need a personal victory. I just wanted to do my best for the team, and for the new team I hoped to build.

I dressed, and Gabriel and I left the gym together. "You're like a dolphin," he said to me as we walked

15

to a coffee shop. "You and the water are natural partners. I don't think I've ever felt as comfortable in any situation in my life as you seem when you're in the pool."

"I could show you," I said.

"No, I like to swim," Gabriel said. "And I'm pretty good at it, but it's not the same."

"I didn't mean that. I meant that I think *we* could be natural partners. If you'll give us a chance."

"Kit, I have to tell you, I think you're too good to be true. You're maybe the handsomest white boy I ever saw; you swim like a merman; you study art—and you're interested in me? What's wrong with this picture?"

"Nothing, actually. Let's complete it," I said.

"I need a little space. I never expected to be swept off my feet like this. You're not part of my plan," he said.

"Oh, yeah, like you have life all figured out while we're both twenty fucking-years old. Twenty-and-a-half, to be more accurate. And you've never even come to my bed. I think we owe it to ourselves to try. If the sex is bad, then I'll surrender. No, that's not true: I refuse to surrender unless you turn out to be a bad lay *and* a bad painter. But until then?"

"Kit Prescott, White Boy Wonder, you're wearing down my resistance," Gabe said.

"Good," I said. "I've probably been really lame about this, but let me try to explain: Never in my life have I wanted anything—or anyone—as much as I want you. Gabriel, I'm handing you my heart. It's yours. If it were only up to me, then I'd want you to take it and be gentle with it. But it's not just up to me. You have to want it, too. I mean us, together. My heart is yours, whichever way it goes."

"Will you give me some time?" he asked.

"How about twenty minutes?"

"How about twenty-four hours?" he asked.

"I'll wait until tomorrow for your answer, but only if you get into my bed tonight. I won't wait any longer for that."

"That's fair," Gabriel said. "I've wanted it, too. But I have to tell you, Kit: I don't think I trust white men. I like them. I sometimes find them attractive," and he indicated me. "But trust? That's a horse of a different color."

"I don't care what color my horse is. I just have to trust him to give me the ride. Gabriel, can you honestly say you see a difference in us?"

"It doesn't matter what I see," he said.

"It's everything, actually," I said. "If you see a deep difference in us because of our skin colors, then I've lost you and my heart."

"It's not like that, Kit," he said. "Other people make those distinctions for us. I don't care about our differences any more than you do. But these things are complicated."

"You mean, like, what to have for dinner?"

"Of course. That's exactly what I meant," Gabriel said.

"Something light, I think, but high in protein. Pizza?"

"Perfect."

Gabriel and I spent the rest of the day together, walking and chattering and laughing and enjoying the last of summer. There was a show I had been wanting to see at the little gallery in the arts wing: Leonard Baskin illustrations. Gabriel wanted to see them, too. We both admired the technique while we wondered at the bleakness of the vision. I still hadn't seen so much as a scrap of Gabe's work. That would have to wait for another day.

And then we went for pizza and a glass of red wine. And a little salad, too, for nutrition's sake. I tried to be as casual as possible, which was not very. The pizza was fine, but I ached for Gabriel, for his hands on my body, for his kiss. I didn't even know, in those days, what else I wanted. I just wanted him. And then we headed back to my little apartment. It was not particularly neat, but at least I had managed to make the bed before I headed out to the swim meet that morning. And the sheets were reasonably clean.

Gabriel had seen me stripped down to my trunks that very afternoon, so there wasn't much in the way of surprise on my side. His body, on the other hand, was still a bit of a mystery to me. Tennis togs can be flattering. Jeans, and sport shirts? Who knows? I dropped everything I was wearing on the floor and waited for him to do the same. And he did. And we faced each other in full birthday suit for the first time. Gabriel was so perfect that I started to cry. He moved forward and reached for me. "What is it, Kit?" he asked.

"Gabe, I'm an idiot," I said as I embraced him. "I knew you were beautiful. And that's why I pursued you this last week. But now that you're finally showing me you, I just . . ." Gabe kissed me. "You asked to see my heart. Well, it's obviously not very strong."

"I suspect you're wrong," he said. "But I also think you should shut up and kiss me again." And I did. Gabriel took my hand and led me to my not-sotidy bed. He sat me on the edge of the bed and then sank to his knees before me. As if he had an extra pair of arms, he managed to envelop me and draw my mouth to his. And then he began to explore my skin. All of it. I had fumbled in bed with lots of boys, lots of times. But I had never experienced a man making love to me. I was gob-smacked.

While Gabriel explored me, I—timidly—began to explore him. Every part of him was luscious. I mostly avoided his dick, to start, not because the size of it frightened me but because I was used to boys, and terrified that he might come suddenly and break the spell. I wasn't ready for it to end. Never have been, actually. I wasn't ready for a lot of things, but others I could handle.

I had never had a man inside me. Boys I tumbled into bed with often wanted *me* inside *them*. And I was happy to oblige. It's a wonderful feeling, being on top. The sense of responsibility is exhilarating. It's like holding another's life in my hands. It's a closeness experienced no other way. But that was about all I knew.

It's also wonderful to submit, I was about to learn—to the right man, of course. And Gabriel is most definitely my right man. I didn't really know what to expect. Surely it would hurt, but how much? Could I take it? Could I welcome this beautiful man into my body, just as easily as I had welcomed him into my heart? What if I hated it? What if I hated him for doing it to me? What if?

Gabriel was wonderfully gentle and patient with me. I realized that I trusted him completely—with my body, with my life, even. When he mounted me, I was ready. And I was his. I surrendered any trace of resistance. There was no change in his embrace and his kiss. There was simply a new bond between us. A new way for us to touch. I felt a thrill of pain, of course. Instinctively I began to breathe deeply. If nothing else, I do know how to breathe. And swimming also taught me to embrace the pain. And within seconds I had accepted him completely. He was in.

I clung to Gabriel as if my life depended on him, as indeed it seemed to. He stroked and petted me and moved inside me carefully and deeply. We neither of us spoke much, although I'm sure I said, "yes" a lot. I got my wish. We shared a long, lovely time together. Unhurried. As if the night were ours alone. But, of course, it couldn't go on forever—as much as I wanted it to—and just as Gabriel was about to fill me with his essence, he whispered in my ear, "Kit, I love you."

If I hadn't been so blissfully flat on my back in that silly bed in that silly little student apartment, I might have reacted to his declaration. But as it was, I simply held him, welcomed his gift, and hoped to keep him inside me forever.

When we came to our senses a bit, I said, "I never made love to an angel before. I don't think I ever made love to a mere mortal either."

"And what's your judgment?" Gabriel asked.

"I want more," I said. "Will you stay over tonight?"

"I'd like to," he said, "very much. But I have such an early morning, really, I have to go."

"Of course," I said. "And tomorrow?"

"I'll be free after two," he said.

"And will you have your answer for me? After two?"

"I thought I gave you my answer, a few minutes ago," he said.

"Gabriel Elijah Williamson, if you're fucking with me, I swear I'll rip your heart right out of your chest!"

"You're showing me a new side of yourself. Did I underestimate my new kitten?"

"Don't!" I said. "Do you really love me?"

"Yes," Gabriel said.

"That's all I need to know. The rest will fall into place." And it did, actually. Not that any of it was easy.

Chapter Three

By the second week in June, after our junior
year, Gabriel was back at his parents' house and
starting a job in construction right away. I was back
at _my_ parents' house and trying to figure out what to
do with myself for the long hot summer. Swimming
at the Y—daily—that was a given. The pool in the
back yard wasn't big enough. No, it had to be the Y
every day. The rest was a bit of a mystery. We had
agreed to talk on the phone every other day. Exactly
at 8:30, I would phone Gabriel's house, so he would
know it was me. And then we would have to figure
out ways to meet. Definitely. But how?

I slept late that Wednesday morning, then slipped
on some shorts and a T-shirt and headed down to
the kitchen. Daddy was at work, of course, and
Momma was out at her regular appointment with her
hairdresser. Esther was busy, as always, but she
ushered me to the breakfast table and said, "Sit
down, Kit. I'll make you some eggs. This is just like
the old days."

I sat down, obediently, and Esther brought me a
cup of coffee. She touched my face and looked down
at me with such tenderness that my eyes welled up.
I was so unused to any real affection in that house.
"I've missed you so much, Essie, I can't even tell
you," I said.

"My little boy is all grown up, now. Tall, and handsome as sin," she said. We both laughed easily. "There's a little ham left from your parents' breakfast, and I'll grill a tomato. You always liked that. You have to tell me what you like to eat these days. I've hardly seen you since last August."

"If it weren't for wanting to see you, I'd probably spend all my time in Chapel Hill," I said. "But anyway, I'm here for the summer, I guess."

Esther threw me one of her disapproving looks, over her shoulder, as she worked on my breakfast.

"Essie, I need your help," I said, as she brought me my plate and joined me at the breakfast table.

"Like you have to ask," she said. "What is it, child?"

"First, I have to tell you something you probably already know. But we've never talked about it."

"And?"

"Your preacher won't approve," I said.

"The Reverend Jones is a fine man. But he doesn't have the only phone line to God."

"Essie, I couldn't bear to lose you," I said.

"Don't be silly, child. What is it?"

"I fell in love," I said.

"Why, Kit, that's wonderful!" she said.

"With a man," I said.

Esther took a moment and then said, "Is this the part where I'm supposed to be shocked? Like I don't understand the ways of the heart?"

"Essie, I fell in love with a *black* man," I said.

"Help me, Jesus!" she said.

I could hear the huge air-conditioning unit in the back yard purring away. The room was mercifully cool. Esther and I sat silently for a while. I finished my breakfast. "I'm waiting for your answer," I said, eventually.

"Don't you high-hand me, little man!" Esther said. "Don't you forget that I fed you and wiped your ass and bounced you on my back and sweated over every fever and held you in my arms when you couldn't sleep, just as if you were my own son. Do you imagine I did all that just so you could throw your life away?"

"Essie, I love him!" I said.

"I did not raise a fool!" she said. "You know as well as I do that races don't mix in this town—in this country—and now you're telling me . . . . Kit, surely you don't think you can live with a colored man— maybe even a *white* man—and not end up dead in a ditch on the edge of town. I couldn't bear it. My heart could not survive that catastrophe. If you told me you wanted to go into your father's business, I would bear it. If you told me you needed to become a feed-and-grain salesman, I would bear it. But this? No, I shall not be moved."

I felt devastated. The one real ally from my childhood just told me I didn't have her support. My very foundations felt shaky. We sat silently for a few minutes, both of us trying to process the situation, I suppose. Eventually I said, "Essie, won't you just meet him?"

"Kit, this is madness," she said. "It makes no difference what I think of him. It's your life we're talking about. Your *life*, child!" and she took my chin in her palm and tweaked it for emphasis. I couldn't think of a thing to say, so I just sat there. Eventually, Esther said, "I've never seen you so determined. If you must, then bring your young man by the house for lunch some afternoon when your Momma is out. And we'll see."

I sprang to life and gave Essie a big hug. "God bless you!" I said, choosing my words for maximum effect. "It'll have to be on a weekend, because he works Monday through Friday."

"That's a good sign," she said. "Sundays are out of the question, of course. But your folks are going to a wedding Saturday-a-week. Bring him then. Around noon. And for God's sake, promise me you'll be careful!"

"Essie, you're my best friend. Always have been," I said.

"Save that soft soap for someone who falls for it," she said.

I gave her a big kiss and then bounded up to my room to get my gym things. Swimming is always my answer—whatever the question.

Gabriel was even more nervous about meeting Esther than I was about the whole thing. I drove over to a gas station on the edge of his neighborhood to pick him up. I hadn't seen him in nearly two weeks, and I was so elated I was vibrating. Kisses were out of the question. Even hugs. He simply slipped into my car and we headed west on the old highway, holding hands. Fortunately, my Oldsmobile could practically drive itself. So one hand on the wheel was more than enough. Gabriel looked wonderful, as always. And he had dressed with care. He didn't have to tell me he was going for "fine young black gentleman." I was so touched he wanted to make a good impression, that it made me love him even more. As if that were possible.

We arrived at the house, and I let us in the back door. The house smelled wonderful. Esther had been cooking for hours, and I felt enveloped by the sheer comfort of it. "Essie, please meet Gabriel Williamson," I said.

"How do you do, Miz Graves?" Gabriel asked. Esther extended her hand and Gabe took it.

"Very well, thanks. And you?" she asked. So far so good. When the introductions were over, Esther led us to the family dining room. She would never have taken a seat at the formal dining table, and this was definitely a family meal for the three of us. I insisted on the family table. She agreed. Esther brought us iced tea, and not the sweet stuff—she knew I hated that. No, just tea and lemon. Perfect. I would have preferred a glass of wine, but that wasn't going to happen that Saturday afternoon.

Esther served us her famous chicken in cream sauce—always my favorite. There was a little bacon in the sauce, which gave it the slightest smoky edge. And she finished it with a handful of green peas, just picked in the garden. Esther's biscuits were flawless—hot and rich and soft as flannel. I almost asked her to teach me how to make them, when I was a teenager. But I had no need for such skills, and it never occurred to me that I might want them in future. It was just as well. It wasn't for me, but at least I'm an accomplished eater.

Lunch went smoothly. I was crossing my fingers. The strawberry pie was delicious. And then, over New Orleans chicory coffee, Esther broached the subject of the business at hand: "Kit, I like your young man," she said, "and I want to thank you for bringing him to meet me. But. . ."

Oh my God! I thought. *Here it comes!*

"I still don't see how you two have the slightest chance at a safe and happy life together," she said. "I don't have to tell you, Mr. Williamson. . .

"Gabriel, please."

"Gabriel, then. You don't need me to tell you how dangerous your relationship is."

"No, you're quite right, of course," Gabriel said. "We're trying to be realistic about it. I'm sure Kit has told you how much we want to be together."

"Yes, and I don't think it's enough."

"Well, we do. But we also know it can't be in Claysville," Gabriel said.

I was nearly as shocked as Esther was. I had *always* known that Gabriel and I would make a home together somewhere else. But we had never actually said it out loud in so many words—that we would be going away. I felt suddenly liberated. "Gabriel loves his family, and I'd hate to lose you, Essie, but we know it has to be . . . somewhere else." There. I said it, too.

"Gabriel, I've loved this boy like my own since the day he was born. I won't see him in harm's way while there's breath left in my body. I refuse to give him up to danger."

"We know the risks. We think we can build a productive—and safe—life together. And we would love to have your blessing," Gabriel said.

There. That was my goal, after all. I had no idea what it was until Gabriel cut through all the drama and got right to it.

"Very well," Esther said. "But if you hurt my boy, I'll come for you. I swear I will!"

"I'd expect nothing less," Gabriel said. "You've not only fed us royally, but you've made us both very happy today, Miz Graves. I don't have words to thank you."

"Don't thank me," she said. "Just have a wonderful future. I always knew my little bird would fly away from me. I'm not stupid. I knew I couldn't keep him. I just didn't think, somehow, that it would be so soon. Well, everything happens in God's time, not mine. I'll pray for you—especially for your safety—every day. Now run along, boys. Kit, your folks will be home in a few hours, and I have a million things to do. Thank God I made enough chicken for their dinner, too."

Gabriel and I skipped up the stairs—hand in hand—to my room. "Kitten, you never told me you grew up in Versailles," he said.

"Don't be dramatic," I said. "It's just a fucking house. I never liked it in the least until you walked in the door." We hung up Gabriel's best suit—carefully—and then fell into bed for some joyous lovemaking. There wasn't much time, but we made the most of it. And then we had to button down our lives again. I drove him back to the east side of town. The glow I felt would have to last for a while. Our next meeting was uncertain. But we made progress that day. Didn't we? And the next? Who knows?

Chapter Four

How could I move forward? Momma and Daddy had to meet Gabriel, too. It was only fair. I wanted to come out of the shadows and into the sunlight. "You told me Gabriel plays tennis? Good," Esther said. "You two plan a game for some Saturday afternoon. You can't take him to the Club, but at the municipal courts it should be okay. I hope. Double-check that. And if it works, then bring Gabriel by the house and I'll give you a glass of iced tea on your way. And you can introduce your school friend to your momma and daddy. _School friend_, mind you. Nothing more. Schools are integrated, after all— more or less—so I can't see any major shock value there."

"Essie, you're so smart," I said. "I wish I took after you more."

"Go along, child," she said. "I don't have time to amuse you just now."

I did leave her to get on with her work, which was considerable. The house was so big that no one person could attend to the whole thing. There were two cleaning women—usually two of them, anyway—who came in every morning to make beds and scrub bathrooms. And in the afternoons they dusted every surface, polished banisters and mirrors, and cleaned chandeliers. The vacuuming alone seemed

31

interminable to me. That was only one reason I escaped the house as often as possible. Every window in the house was washed—inside and out—at least every month. More often when there was the slightest smudge. From grade-school on I was spared the sight of most of the process, except in summer.

There was always a man to do yard work and to help with heavy cleaning projects in the house. Plus an extra man when anything serious needed doing. And there was a laundress who came every Monday, and I'm not talking about sheets and towels and tablecloths and napkins: Washing and ironing them was the responsibility of the women who cleaned the house. No, the Monday laundress was there to see that Momma's clothes were always perfect. And she also pressed a week's worth of dress shirts for Daddy and me. She got the starch just right every time— the shirts floated on the body with perfect crispness, and yet there was no sensation of stiffness whatsoever. I don't know how she did it. We wore pressed shirts to school from junior-high on, in those days, in Claysville. And I'll confess I've never felt quite so well groomed as I did back then.

Esther was in charge of the whole show, and she was stern. Workers either produced or they were out. These were pretty good jobs for the poor people on the east side of town, so there were always others ready to fill any vacancy. Some of the workers in the house were personable, but there was no way I could form a real relationship with any of them. No, Esther was it. She was my bedrock. She had a kitchen helper—who mostly prepped and cleaned—but Esther cooked nearly every morsel of food that went into our mouths. There was extra help when

Momma and Daddy had parties, of course, but day-to-day it was really all about Esther.

Gabriel agreed to the tennis afternoon. He was a bit apprehensive, but I was insistent. And I did, of course, double-check the race policy at the public courts. This was the first time, I think, I ever had to ask any gatekeeper, "Do you admit black people?" and then listen to the "Yes," reply—it was, after all, the law of the land—and *then* have to discern whether it was the truth or not. If I had thought for an instant that Gabriel would be uncomfortable, I would have called it off. But it felt like a go.

I drove right up in front of Gabriel's parents' house that time. We couldn't have him walking to the gas station in tennis whites. It made no sense. Neighborhood kids seemed to materialize out of no-where to admire my—almost—muscle car. It wasn't the souped-up version of the Oldsmobile Cutlass, but it was impressive none the less. Gabriel's little brother and his sister walked out to the driveway, shyly, to meet me. I got out of the car and shook their hands. They were both of them so beautiful and so like Gabriel that I started to cry, just a little, behind my sunglasses.

I sensed that Gabriel's mother pulled back the front curtain just enough to peer out at the man who was taking her son away. No, I didn't just sense it: I *felt* it. I know she looked out at us. And I wanted to be worthy. I wanted to be the one who could create a home for him and keep him safe. I wanted her to know that I would cherish him. I wanted a lot, but mostly I felt like an idiot. We slipped into my car, I started it and put it in reverse, and only then did the local kids begin to disperse. I was so careful. If I had hit one of them—even a tap—it would have been not only terrible but also the end of Gabriel and me, I feared. I felt all the responsibility. We headed to the west side of town.

When I pulled into the driveway, I headed to the back where I always parked. And just across the lawn I spied the little assembly that was already giving me butterflies. "Momma, Daddy, this is Gabriel Williamson. From UNC."

"How do you do, Miz Prescott, Mr. Prescott," Gabriel asked. They shook his hand. Both of them. Momma was always gracious, and Daddy went right into his hale-fellow-well-met pose. It looked as if things might be going well. But really? It was too early to tell. Esther arrived with a big pitcher of iced tea and plenty of glasses and ice. She also produced a little pitcher of sugar syrup for the sweet teeth in the mix. And lots of lemon slices. I greeted Esther, of course, but she and Gabriel did not acknowledge each other. The whole thing began to seem so unremarkable that I started to relax a bit.

"Why, Gabriel, I'm so glad you've got Kit playing tennis again," Momma said. "He was always so good at it, and yet he hasn't been on a court since I don't know when."

"Miz Prescott, I have to tell you he's a natural player. And his backhand is a real challenge to me.

But I usually beat him. So that's why he's my favorite opponent. He keeps me on my toes." *Okay, Gabriel,* I thought. *You don't have to lay it on so thick.*

Momma slipped right into Southern Belle mode: "I can see you have the hands for it," she said. "My father played tennis, too. He was a state doubles champion. My, it all seems so long ago now."

I decided to nip that conversation in the bud. "What's this about a new city reservoir?" I asked Daddy. "What's wrong with the old one?"

He warmed to the topic, as I knew he would. And when Daddy spoke, everyone listened. "Kit, you never understood how this town is growing. You always had your nose buried in books instead of looking around you at all the possibilities, and the opportunities." I listened to some more of that for a while and then steered the conversation toward the fact that Gabriel and I had reserved a court and needed to leave right away to make it on time.

The good-byes went smoothly, and then the tennis boys slipped into my car and headed off to the municipal courts. Once we were on the road, I said to Gabriel, "What is this 'Miz Prescott, I have to tell you he's a natural player,' routine? You never wooed me like that."

"I never had to. *You* wooed *me*, remember?"

"True. But you're good at it. I wouldn't mind a little attention like that," I said.

"I want to give you all the attention you can stand, Kitten. But not here. Not in Claysville. It's just wrong. Don't you feel it? Let's play tennis. Let's get through this afternoon. Let's get through this summer. Let's get back to Chapel Hill where we can at least breathe. And then we'll figure it out. You know we will," Gabriel said.

"You always were smarter than I am," I said. "Yes, we'll figure it out, Angel. But not today. Meanwhile, let's find out if my backhand is really as formidable as you say. I'm feeling it."

We played for an hour or so—just enough to make our court reservation look legit. It was fun, of course. Because we were together. Being *in bed* together would have been a whole lot more satisfying, but it didn't seem to be a possibility just then. We shared sets. I was in good form. He was the better player, but I felt so strong, just being with him, that I topped my usual game. And then we decided to get something to eat.

"We could be in Chapel Hill in maybe forty minutes, or even less. What do you say?" I asked Gabriel.

"I say, 'Drive fast, but safely.' How's that?"

"Good answer," I said, and headed for the Interstate. "I really am hungry, but I want you in my bed even more. How are we going to work this?"

"How about takeout?" Gabriel suggested.

"I told you you're smarter than I am. Dewey's is on the way." We picked up a barbecue dinner and got to my little apartment in less than an hour. It was a challenge—getting our tennis whites hung up carefully so we wouldn't look too disheveled later— but we managed it. And then we sat in bed and gobbled down just enough barbecue and coleslaw and hush puppies to fortify us for monumental lovemaking. It was maybe the unexpectedness of it that helped to make it so joyous. And when I came I thought I might explode. Hey, what a way to go! And I don't think Gabriel and I ever laughed so much as we did that silly evening.

The drive back to Claysville was less jubilant. Somber realities were waiting for both of us. I dropped Gabriel in front of his parents' house and headed back to mine.

I parked in my usual spot and let myself in the back door. I hoped to make it up to my room without detection, but there were lights on, and Momma was sitting in the breakfast room playing solitaire. "Kit, darling," she called out. "Come, talk to me." I did, of course. I joined her at the table. "Would you like some coffee? Or how about a glass of Madeira?"

"That sounds perfect, Momma. And one for you?"

"Why not?" she said. I poured two little glasses of dessert wine and brought them to the table. "Thank you, dear," Momma said. "We loved meeting your school friend today."

"Oh, good," I said. "Gabriel enjoyed meeting you, too."

"He's very attractive," she said. I didn't quite know how to react. It felt like a minefield.

"Smart, too," I said. "And talented. His paintings are so beautiful! Well, maybe you'll get to see them some time. And he's a hell of a tennis player. Much better than I ever was."

"Kit, your daddy and I want only what's best for you. We want you to be happy. We want you to be safe. And we wonder if you having a colored friend is the best choice."

"Momma, I can't listen to this. You met Gabriel. You know he's a quality guy. And he's my best friend. Could we leave it at that for tonight?" I asked.

"Yes, of course," she said. "But your daddy wants to talk to you."

"He's still up?" I asked.

I hadn't been summoned to "the study" since the time in fifth grade I got caught cheating on a math test. *Helping* is really what I was trying to do. I never had any trouble with the answers, but classmates did. Anyway, it was a major Citizenship violation, and punishments were assigned. I didn't care half as much as Daddy did, not that he held himself to such high scruples. He was stern. I tried to look contrite. And now?

I rapped softly on his door. "Come in, Kit," he said, and I entered. It would have been a wonderful room if it had occupied his soul; if he had read the books on his shelves. But don't get me started. That is not where this story needs to go.

"Hi, Daddy," I said. "Momma said you want to talk to me."

"Yes, son. Sit down. Would you like a cigar? No, of course. Swimming and all. But how about a cognac?"

"Sure," I said. And I couldn't tell whether the evening was becoming interesting or terrifying. I still felt Gabriel's kisses on my lips and his body all over mine. It helped. Daddy handed me a snifter of brandy that was too generous, but I simply accepted it and thanked him. "What did you want to talk about?" I asked. I don't always get right to the point, but that evening I did.

"We haven't seen much of you this summer. We're concerned about your future. One more year at Carolina and then what?"

"Well, I'm not certain, but my grades are good, and I'll graduate next June, maybe with honors. There are companies that need my skills—museums, cities, cultural institutions, auction houses. There's work out there."

"Kit, I always hoped you'd take over my business some day," he said.

"Daddy, we've talked about this before. You know it's not for me. I understand that it's what you love, but it's just not for me. Please don't ask me again. I can't, I won't change my mind," I said.

"I'll give you one thing, son, you've always stood your ground. Even in your playpen, you never gave an inch."

"Like father, like son," I said. It was thorny, but I also felt a certain amount of pride in it. And I hoped—sincerely—that he would too.

"About that friend of yours," Daddy said.

"His name is Gabriel, Daddy," I said.

"I don't like him. I don't want you to see him anymore."

"I didn't expect you to fall in love with a black man," I said. Perhaps the cognac was cutting in. "But I hoped you'd be respectful and let it go at that."

"It's not because he's colored," Daddy said. "You know we're not prejudiced." I choked back every rejoinder that surged up from my heart. I sat. I waited. "I just don't think you should be around him. I think he's queer."

And then all hell broke loose. I sprang to my feet and screamed, "How dare you speak to me that way! You have no right to say that about my friend!"

"I'll say whatever I like in my own home," Daddy said. "And I can't see why you're so upset, unless, of course, you're queer, too."

"As a matter of fact," I said, "I am. And proud of it." And from there it got worse. The Prescott males had butted heads for years, of course. That's how family works. But this time it grew so heated that we both said things we knew we'd regret. Until finally Daddy said, "Get out of my sight! You're no son of mine!"

"Correct," I said. "And I'll go gladly." Momma was standing right by the study door as I left. She knew, of course, what had happened.

"Kit, darling," she said. I kept moving. I ran up the stairs to my room and threw some things into a suitcase. Then I dumped it into the back of my car and headed to I-85 as fast as I safely could. Daddy had bought me that Oldsmobile the year before. Midnight blue. Convertible. They drove Cadillacs, Momma and Daddy, but the young son-and-heir should be seen in something a little sportier. I liked my car—the same as I liked a lot of my privileges—but that night, as I sped toward what felt like freedom in Chapel Hill, with the wind in my hair, I said to myself, *This car is so stupid. I will never put the top down again. I would leave it in a ditch somewhere if I could, but I can't. I just want to move on. And as soon as Gabriel and I find our own way, then I'll drop this heap like a hot potato.*

Momma called me that afternoon and said, "Kit, darling, he didn't mean it."

"Momma, he meant every word," I said.

"Will you come back home for August?" she asked.

"I can't, Momma. Thank you for trying. I'd like to, for your sake." I didn't mention that another month with Esther would have been precious. "But I can't spend another day under that man's roof." Highfalutin words, indeed, from a boy with no visible means of support. Not only had I never missed a meal, but I had never honestly considered how to make my own way in the world.

"We'll talk about it again, soon," she said. "But I don't want you to worry. Your tuition is paid for your senior year, and I'll send you what you need for your rent and all. Kit, promise me you'll try to forgive him. I know it's a lot to ask. But we love you, and we only want what's best for you."

"Momma, what's best for me is Gabriel. And I can't see how that's going to work in Claysville. I love you, Momma," I said. I wasn't entirely certain how deeply I believed that, but I knew it needed to be said.

Chapter Five

Our senior year was filled with getting good grades and thinking about the future, of course, and making love as often as possible. Gabriel moved into my little apartment, and that gave him a bit more pocket money from the tiny stipend his church had granted him. I might have envied him his self-sufficiency, had I not had a clear eye toward the privilege of my situation. I assumed it couldn't last, but I decided to use my birthright as long as I could hold onto it.

That winter I heard about a job fair for art history majors. Museums and cultural institutions—even the auction houses—were coming from all over the country with presentations to explain their missions and, just perhaps, to woo candidates for low-level jobs. Low-paying jobs. But that was standard in the arts, in those days, at least.

I told Gabriel about the fair. He said, "Kitten, you go for it. Take whatever feels right. I can paint anywhere. It's really up to you."

"You'd follow me to Kalamazoo?"

"I'd follow you to Nome."

"How about Natchez?"

"Now you're testing me."

"How about New York?"

"If it's what you want. I've had a little dream, since childhood, really, about living in a loft in Greenwich Village with a hot guy who loves me. I always knew I could paint there, that I could do my best work there. I just didn't know how to do it. And I didn't know you."

Just before I fell asleep that night, with Gabriel's body pressed against mine, I said to myself, *Kit Prescott, you have never had a proper dream in your entire life. All you've ever wanted is to swim, and to be loved by the right man. And now you have both. And that man has a* genuine *dream. And it's up to you. Make it happen!*

I scheduled some appointments. The Metropolitan was my first choice. The Whitney was also on the schedule. And the Modern. And the Frick. I decided against interviewing with Sotheby's and Christie's. I had nothing against commerce—my whole life had been supported by it. I simply decided since choices had to be made, I wanted to focus on the nonprofit sector. And since whatever little job I might land would be largely nonprofit, I might as well be all in.

I dressed carefully for the interviews, in a navy blazer and a white shirt with a rep tie and gray flannel slacks. My résumé was impeccably constructed and printed. I showed up. I smiled a lot. I knew enough about Gabriel's charm to know that there are different ways to approach men and women. Gay men? Straight men? Gay women? Straight women? It can be confusing. But I worked it, the best I could. I actually worked it better than I had ever worked any situations except my best swim competitions, maybe. And landing Gabriel, of course. That was my best work. But I did what needed to be done, and then I let go of it.

I was used to life being relatively easy, and so when the scout from the Met called me and asked me to come back the next day, I was not shocked. And when he said, "We can offer you a junior position in American Paintings," I simply said, "When would you like me to start?"

"Would June 20th work for you?"

"Perfect," I said. We shook hands on the deal, and then I floated home. Gabriel was out, at a class. I was vibrating with excitement. Was it for me? Was it for him? Perhaps it was for *us*. I paced the little apartment for nearly an hour until he returned.

"I'm thinking if we leave on June 8th, right after graduation," I said to Gabriel, "we should get there in time to settle in. Does that work for you?"

"You're being mysterious, Kitten. Please include me in this conversation."

"Greenwich Village, here we come!" I said, and grabbed him in a fierce embrace.

"Shit! You didn't! Where?"

"The Metropolitan Museum of Art," I answered grandly.

"Fuck! Kit Prescott, is there no end to what you can do?"

"None," I said. "And you'd best not forget it!"

We danced around for a bit, and then put on our coats and headed out for a celebratory dinner. It was heady stuff, the concept of making our escape.

Gabriel, certainly, had no illusions about our future being easy. I, on the other hand, had no interest at all in negativity. I had a fellow art history major I liked, very much. There weren't many. He was from New York City, and though I didn't really know him well, I had admired his spirit—his *chutzpah*—since we met the year before. Gabe and I had coffee with him one afternoon in the spring.

"Jerry, what are you doing after graduation?" I asked.

"I didn't tell you?"

"Not a word."

"Well, it pales in comparison to your coup, but I got a little job at the Brooklyn Museum."

"Shit! Jerry! I had no idea. That's wonderful! Even *I* know the Brooklyn Museum has some of the finest holdings in African and Egyptian Art in the country. And the pre-Columbian collection? Those Andean weavings alone are so precious—Gabriel, will you stop me, or will I keep blathering on?"

"You blather all you like, Kitten," he said.

"Thanks, Kit," Jerry said. "I'm really happy about it, too. So, what are your plans?"

"We're going to drive up the day after graduation. And then we have to find a place to stay. Any suggestions?" I asked.

"Yes, as a matter of fact. I know a cheap little hotel—almost a flophouse, really—where you could probably stay for a week or so, until you find an apartment. I'll write down the information. It's in a fairly nice part of the Village. I think you'll like the neighborhood, and it's a good place to base yourselves while you look around.

"Apartment-hunting in New York City sounds a little daunting," Gabriel said.

"Don't sweat it," Jerry said. "You'll buy the *Times* and check out the Classifieds. And you'll wander around until you find the area you like best. And you might even see listings on lampposts, or on bulletin boards in laundromats. Ask at neighborhood bars, too. You never know."

"I'm not going to worry about it," I said. Was that the truth?

"Don't," Jerry said. "Just do it. You'll be fine."

"Thanks, Jerry," I said. "You've been a big help."

"Don't mention it. I'll give you my parents' phone number, so you can reach me. I have to go hunting for a place of my own, too. We can compare notes."

"Perfect," I said. "Thanks again!"

I was apprehensive about graduation and all the Claysville issues it stirred up. After some thought, I phoned Momma and told her I wasn't going. "It's not mandatory, so I'll be driving to New York as soon as classes are finished," I said.

"Kit, darling," she said. "I've been looking forward to watching you graduate for ages. I'm not certain about your daddy, but I intend to be there."

"Thank you, Momma," I said, "but I'm firm about this. No ceremony. Off to New York. I'll phone you as soon as we get there and tell you how to reach me. And don't worry about anything. We'll be fine."

"Of course I'll worry, but drive safely, and call me just as soon as you can."

"I will, Momma," I said. "I love you." And it was time to hang up.

Gabriel's situation was quite different. He was the first in his generation to graduate from college, so it was a big fucking deal for the whole family. About twenty of them were driving over from Claysville that morning, with another dozen or so from his church. It would be an all-day thing for him, and for me—by extension. I had only just met Gabriel's brother and sister, and only briefly. I had no idea what to expect from the rest of the family. Gabriel assured me that everyone would be gracious. He *didn't* say, "They'll love you just as much as I do." That would have been over the top. Our relationship was more honesty-based than that. But he asked me to relax and try to enjoy the day.

We were seated separately. Alphabetically, I suppose, or by major, or however they did it. It was a big class. Just before we had to take our seats, Gabriel showed me where his family was, so I'd know where to find him afterward. I looked over at them during the very dreary commencement address. *How different*, I thought, *from my family*. I had a few aunts and uncles and cousins. All the time I was growing up I saw little in the way of genuine affection among any of them. I just didn't get it, the concept of family. But Gabriel had a real one, and I was about to be immersed in it. And I was not exactly terrified, but? We received our diplomas.

Graduations bring out the best in everyone, I think. So much hard work. So many dreams. So much promise. Gabriel's parents were beaming with pride, of course. They greeted me warmly. His father smiled broadly as he shook my hand, and his mother actually kissed my cheek. Gabriel's brother and sister were just as charming and beautiful as they were at our first, brief meeting. I got hugs from some of the aunts and church ladies. The uncles and churchmen were a bit more reserved. Skeptical, even. But no one refused my hand.

There were cousins, too. And they were just like kids everywhere, of course: Most of them didn't want to be there, and even the ones who did were restless. One girl, maybe fifteen, grabbed my hand and said, "Hi, I'm Sarah. You should come to the picnic with me."

"Hi, Sarah, I'm Kit," I said. "Thanks for the invitation. Let me check with Gabriel and see what the plans are." When I finally got a chance to speak to Gabriel, I said to him, "You have a new rival for my affections," indicating Sarah, whose eyes were fixed on us.

"She's a spitfire," he said, "but you could do worse."

"Help!" I said.

Gabriel laughed and said, "The Prescott stud is afraid of a pretty little filly? Don't worry, Kitten, I'll protect you."

"Thanks, Angel," I said. "What's next?"

There was, indeed, a picnic in the park nearby. The ladies quickly set up a wonderful feast with all my Southern favorites: fried chicken, of course; deviled eggs; baked beans that held the heat, as if by magic, as did the macaroni-and-cheese; various slaws and salads with cabbage and beans and potatoes, and even an okra salad that was like nothing I've tasted, before or since. There were chicken livers wrapped in bacon. There were some other pork parts I've never fully understood. Corn bread and iced tea, of course.

The entire party was about Gabriel, but I was there, too. And I was having a good time. I watched him interact with them all. I tried my best to relax into the situation. Gabriel owed his full attention to the friends and family who had supported him all his life. He understood. He gave back. He also tried to include me, as much as possible. But it was up to me to be a good guest. And I do know how to give good guest. I worked it, with an open heart.

Late in the afternoon, two of Gabriel's boy cousins lured me away from the picnic to a spot behind the little brick structure that housed bathrooms. They were there to smoke cigarettes, mostly. That didn't interest me, but when they offered to spike my tea with something clear from a flask, I was happy to accept. It was all great fun until one of them kissed me, and I had to go into damage control mode. "Thank you, James," I said. "You're a very handsome guy, but I'm committed." It worked, I think. They laughed and moved on to other diversions on that beautiful June afternoon.

"Angel," I said that evening after we had finished all the festivities and good-byes, "thank you for including me."

"Shut up, Kitten!" he said. "We're in this together, aren't we? It's really for *me* to thank *you* for joining in, for accepting my family and friends, warts and all."

"I like them so much!" I said. "Even your Uncle Ruben. He wanted to hate me—I could see it in his eyes—and yet, when we spoke . . . " I got a little weepy. Gabriel reached for me. I fell into his arms. I took a deep breath and said, "He asked me my intentions, more or less. I looked at him squarely and said, 'Gabriel is the finest and the most talented man I've ever met. I intend to honor him for the rest of my life.' "

"Shit!" Gabriel said. "And what did Uncle Ruben say?"

"He said, 'See that you do!' And then he shook my hand. Let's get some rest, Angel," I said. "We have a long drive tomorrow."

"I'm not so sure I'll sleep tonight," Gabriel said. "I'm even more excited about our adventure than I expected to be."

"Since I'll probably do most of the driving then I'd better sleep for both of us," I said. "But first I need some expert relaxation therapy. Give me a double, Doc."

Gabriel took me in his arms and gave me exactly what I needed. As always. And after I came, I slept like a baby right up until the alarm jangled us in the morning. I think Gabriel slept, too. It was, in some ways, the last sleep of our childhoods.

Chapter Six

We drove to New York in my Oldsmobile. Top up all the way. We had some clothes and Gabriel's satchel with painting supplies. A few books. Not much else. We checked into the cheap hotel Jerry had suggested. It was grim but reasonably clean. I found a parking garage a block away. And then we went out for a meal. There was a little French restaurant nearby. We looked at the menu and looked at each other, and said, in unison, "Yes."

The next morning I found an Oldsmobile dealership in the Yellow Pages. I didn't care what transportation needs might arise—losing that car was my first priority. The dealership was in midtown, way over on the West Side, almost on the Hudson. "We don't get that much call for convertibles—not like down South," the dealer said. "But some guy from Westchester will want it. I could take it. I'll give you $1000."

I hesitated. Surely Daddy had paid at least $5000 for it. It was "loaded"—leather interior, power windows, air conditioning, V-8 turbo-God-knows-what transmission. Everything worked perfectly, even the clock. And the ashtrays had never been used. But it did have just over two years on it. I didn't know what to do. Gabriel couldn't really help me with the decision. I hemmed and hawed a bit, and then the salesman said, "$1250, take it or leave it."

"Ill take it," I said. It was as if a great weight had been lifted. As Gabriel and I headed back to the hotel—cash stuffed in our pockets—I began to feel our adventure had really begun.

We followed Jerry's advice and bought a copy of *The New York Times*. The classified apartment listings were confusing. I headed out to a little stationery shop for a street map. That helped. We penciled in an area bounded by 14th Street and Christopher Street, north and south, and then Greenwich Avenue to the east, roughly, and Hudson Street to the west. We felt better already. And then we started our search.

After a week of phone calls—often with bogus leads—we decided we had seen enough fifth-floor walk-ups with the bathroom across the hall. And we started pounding the pavement, stopping to look at laundromats and other community bulletin boards. I had no problem talking to strangers, and all the locals we encountered went out of their way to be helpful. "Nice town," I said, and Gabriel beamed despite the effort and uncertainty.

After a few days of searching on foot, we happened upon a notice taped to a lamppost. "Large studio, sunny, quiet building, available immediately." I phoned from a booth on the corner, and the man who answered invited us to come right over, to a building on Bank Street. For the first time we were filled with real hope.

Karl Nesbitt greeted us at the door and invited us in. He was an older guy, pleasant looking but a little sad. "It's just on the floor above, in the front. Gets lots of sunlight. The guy who lived here last is an actor, and he just got a national tour. So he moved out this morning, and you're the first ones to see it. I haven't really had time to look it over, but I think the room's probably neat enough for you to get an idea if it's for you or not. Come on up."

We followed Karl upstairs and he let us in. The room contained a bed, a kitchen table with chairs, and not much else. But it did have a real bathroom with a big tub. Definitely a plus. It didn't take long for Gabriel and me to look it over and look at each other with total affirmation. "I think it's just what we need," I said.

"Good," Karl said. "I just made some coffee, so why don't you come downstairs, and I'll give you a cup. And we can talk." We followed him down to his apartment, the big one on the ground floor with several rooms, a big kitchen, and the garden in back. Karl's apartment was filled with pictures and books and big comfortable furniture that had obviously seen a lot of living. He ushered us into the breakfast area and poured us coffee in English china cups. I had never felt more welcome.

"You boys don't sound like New Yorkers. What's your story?" Karl asked. I gave him the capsule version: recent graduates of UNC, my new little job at the Met starting soon, Gabriel's plan to find something as soon as we settled. Karl seemed satisfied that we were an okay risk, I guessed—one of us employed for certain, the other charming and well-spoken. "The rent is $200 a month. Does that work for you?"

We gulped a little, and looked at each other for confirmation. "Tell you what," Karl said. "Why don't we make it $150 a month for the first six months, and then $200 after that.

"Mr. Nesbitt, that's really generous of you," I said.

"Call me Karl. I have a simple lease form. If you'll fill in your names, we can get this finished right now."

"Perfect," I said. We added our names to the form, then signed and dated it. Karl did the same. And it was done. "First and last months' rent?" I asked. I had done some homework on this stuff.

"Yes, please," Karl said. I peeled off $350 from our dwindling reserve and handed it to him. And then Gabriel and I could relax a bit.

"Great coffee," I said. I hope you'll tell us where you buy it."

"Of course. Ask me anything you want to know about the neighborhood."

"How long have you lived here?" Gabriel asked.

"My parents bought this building in the '20s— that's the 1920s, not the 1820s." We laughed. "So I spent part of my childhood here. And then I went off to college—to Brown, actually—where I met a lovely guy and planned to move to San Francisco with him. But then the war broke out, and I enlisted in the Army Signal Corps. I guess they didn't see me as a soldier any more than I did, so I ended up spending the whole war working at the training center in New Jersey. And then, after the war, I felt New York calling me back. By then, my parents were getting on in years, so I took a room upstairs—your room actually—and stayed around to help out. And then the building passed to me. I had some happy memories of the place, so I moved into this apartment, and I've been here ever since."

"It's very inviting," I said.

"Thank you. I do like my comforts. I probably shouldn't tell you this, since we don't know each other well, but I have a sister in Connecticut who's been asking me for years to move into her country house. I love my sister, but I don't know about living with her. I'm guessing I could tolerate her for about half the year, as long as I had a home to come back to.

"What I'm saying is, if you boys take to this neighborhood and this building—and I suspect you will—then maybe next year you could switch apartments with me. I haven't had a dinner party in six months, and I rarely sit in the garden. I don't need all of this anymore. Especially if I'm spending all that time in Connecticut. But that's a ways off. Meanwhile, move in as soon as you like. The bed and the table-and-chairs are mine, so you're welcome to use them. Otherwise, I'll have my handyman take them out."

"Karl, we'll be happy to use them. We didn't bring much more than the clothes on our backs. So it's a comfort to know that—no matter what—we'll be able to sleep and eat."

"And make love," Karl said.

"And make love," I affirmed. Karl gave us each a front-door key and a room key, and then Gabriel and I repeated our thank-yous and headed back to the hotel. Within a few hours we had checked out and ferried our meager quantity of stuff to Karl's building. It was perhaps the most joyous moment of our lives together since we fell in love, embracing our new love-nest. We celebrated with a bottle of champagne.

Maybe two days later I was cleaning and organizing when I decided to buy a few bed and bath linens of our own. Gabriel was out, on a job interview, and I was trying to get as much done as possible in the next two days before my job started. I rapped softly on Karl's door, hating to disturb him. He opened the door seconds later and said, "Kit! What a nice surprise. Come in." I followed him obediently and sat down at the breakfast table. He poured me a coffee, as before, and one for himself. "How do you like the Village, so far?" he asked.

"We love it. We keep pinching ourselves to make sure we're not dreaming it."

"It's real, all right. I suspect you already feel the pull of New York City, the way I always did. And the Village is a lovely place to live. You'll see. What can I do for you?"

"I nearly forgot. I'm trying so hard to get us settled before I start work in two days, and I wondered where I should go for some linens," I said.

"There's a very nice boutique nearby, but it can be expensive. Why not go to Macy's? They have a huge selection. Some of it's shoddy and some of it's just fine. I'm guessing you can tell the difference. I'm guessing you're used to the good stuff," Karl said.

"In another life," I said. "Karl, why are you so kind to us?"

Karl was quiet for a moment, and then he answered, "There is a reason, actually. You see, I had a Gabriel of my own, a long time ago. It was difficult; very difficult. I'm not dismissing the challenges interracial couples face today—far from it. But it began to feel impossible back then. His name was Johnny. And when Johnny held me in his arms, nothing else mattered. But when he wasn't holding me in his arms, we had to figure out how to live in Whitey's world.

"I didn't care about the restaurants where the two of us were unwelcome. I didn't care about the looks we got when we were out together. I could ignore the slights and subtle insults. Even the blatant ones. I made a home for Johnny here, so we never had to worry about where to live, whether we could get a lease. I didn't care, but Johnny did. It broke him. He decided to return to his hometown in Alabama. Without me. And I let him go. Have I forgiven myself for that, in all these years? Never. I felt such a failure. Then as now. How could I be so weak that I couldn't make a safe world for my beloved and me? I've been asking myself that question ever since."

Karl and I were quiet for a bit. "Kit, don't make my mistake," he said. "I looked at you two when you showed up a few mornings ago, and your story was as clear as your faces are pretty. It's going to be mostly up to you, Kit, to make this work. You're tough as granite. I knew that instantly. Growing up with privilege has its rewards. I had a small dose of that, too. So I know. Gabriel hasn't gotten this far without some backbone, that's certain. But you're going to have to be the steel in it. You'll always rise to the top like the cream, but a smart, talented, beautiful black man who wants to become a great artist? *It's different.* Call me racist, but I don't think he can do it alone. I think it's up to you."

"Shit! Karl, you're scaring me," I said.

"I doubt that Kit Prescott scares easily. And that's a good thing," Karl said. "I just want you to promise me you'll be very good to each other and that you understand your mission. Now, run along, young man. You have work to do, and I have a life, in case you didn't notice." I rose and embraced him, and Karl hugged me back. I hated to let go. He offered me the embrace I never got from Daddy. And I started to cry. "Now, now," Karl said. "We can't have you turn into a weepy old man. There's plenty of time for that in the future, believe me. Macy's. Herald Square. Take the 1, 2, or 3 at 14th Street, whichever arrives first. Get out at 34th Street, and you're only one long block away. Happy hunting!" And I was off on another adventure.

I told Gabriel about my day, of course, and what I had learned about Karl's past. But I never told Gabe about Karl's admonition. I couldn't have said the words even, in those days. I just tucked it all away in my heart—like the Virgin Mary, I thought.

Chapter Seven

I started my new job at the Metropolitan. I liked it. Some of the staffers were wary, but most of them were welcoming. And right away I discovered the McBurney YMCA on 14th Street. It had a big pool, and it was only a few blocks away from the apartment. Perfect. Gabriel's adjustment to our new life was not quite so easy. But a few months into my new job I happened to hear about an opening in the conservation department. It seemed to me that Gabriel was just right for it, and so I suggested he interview.

"Kitten, thank you," he said, "but I'll find something. You don't need to worry about me."

"No, of course I don't need to worry about you," I said, "because I know you'll interview for this job. And you'll get it, because you have just the skills they need, and because it will teach you more about paint and canvas and board and marble than you could ever learn in any school. And you'll get the job because it's exactly what you need to be doing at this moment in time."

This was not the first time, of course, that I had asserted—strongly—that something-or-other should happen. And it was not the first time that Gabriel had resisted. But I was often right, and he was always willing to admit it. "Come to me, Kitten," he said. "Who should I call?" I gave him the particulars, and he phoned the next morning.

Gabriel got an interview and prepared for it. This time, "fine young black gentleman" was not his selling point, of course. This time he was going for "highly skilled young art student with a scholarly interest in restoration." And he got the job! I knew he would, of course. Or at least I *prayed* he would, for his ego's sake. No, for his future's sake. Our future's sake. And then we both had jobs that would keep a roof over our heads, food in our bellies, and a sense of purpose in our days.

The next year, Karl did decide to divide his time between Bank Street and his sister's house in Connecticut. And so he swapped apartments with us. It was too good to be true, and yet it was true. And Karl seemed pleased that we were there, and solid, and responsible for his property. I told him I was most certainly not a gardener, and he promised that his handyman would maintain the garden with the least intrusion on our lives. Or whatever level of intrusion we wanted, considering the handyman was one hot piece of work.

An old building needs constant maintenance, so Javier was around nearly every weekday. And he was very friendly. Javier had a great smile and an easy, flirtatious way about him. Gabriel and I considered inviting Javier into our bed. "What do you think, Angel?" I asked Gabriel. "Do we need some recreation?"

"I don't need anything but you, Kitten. But I think we should do whatever you want. Decide for both of us, and I'll be happy with your decision, either way."

I liked Gabriel's reply. I liked the responsibility. "Let me think about it for a minute," I said. "We've never done anything like this. The fact that we're even talking about it suggests it might be something we need to try. But then, why, really?"

"Because sex is fun, I guess. No other reason. Don't fret about it, Kitten. Yes or no, it's not a big deal," Gabriel said.

I did fret about my decision, for nearly a week. And then finally I said, "Let's see if Javier is free after work tomorrow."

"Sure," Gabriel said.

And the decision was made. I relaxed a bit. The next morning as I left the apartment to head to work, Javier was already on the job. "Javier, if you're free this evening, why don't you stop in after work and have a little supper with us? It won't be much, but I'm pretty good at phoning for takeout."

"Thanks, Kit," Javier said. "What can I bring?"

"Just yourself," I said, observing his hard, tan limbs and imagining the rest of his tightly muscled body. "About 7:00?"

"Perfect," Javier said, and flashed me his delicious grin.

And I was off to work. Was I apprehensive about my decision? Yes, but there was no turning back now. And so I put it out of my mind, mostly, and got on with my day. At lunchtime I phoned Gabriel to tell him our evening was a go. "Sounds like fun," he said. And I was satisfied that the whole thing was properly light and inconsequential.

Javier showed up, a few minutes early, with a bottle of red wine and a little bunch of flowers from the garden. He scrubbed his hands thoroughly at the kitchen sink, and then we sat down to the Chinese takeout meal I had ordered. Hot-and-sour soup, sesame seef, chicken with broccoli, that sort of thing. "How long have you worked for Karl?" I asked.

"It's more than five years now," Javier said. "Nice guy. He's always been very generous with me."

"And with us, too," I said, indicating the comfortable apartment where we sat. We raised a glass to Karl and thanked him for his generosity, and then we got down to the business at hand.

"I should take a quick shower," Javier said. "I'm sure I stink."

"You smell fine to me," Gabriel said.

"And to me," I said. Javier, overruled, followed us to the bedroom. His kisses were good. Not Gabriel's, but good. We got out of our clothes and fell into bed together. Javier's lean body was even nicer than I had imagined, and he shared it freely. The muskiness he had acquired in a day of labor added a powerful aphrodisiac to the mix. The three of us embraced and tasted each other. It was free and passionate. It was delicious.

Javier was keen to top me. I was a little apprehensive. No one but Gabriel had ever been there. It wasn't the size of Javier's dick that gave me pause—generous as it was. If I could take Gabriel, then I could take any man. It was just that my ass had always belonged to Gabriel. And now? What were we doing? But this was no time for prudery. I embraced the situation and surrendered. Javier's work-hardened hands on my body felt new and different. I welcomed his embrace. I welcomed him inside me. It was good. Different, but good.

Gabriel moved into position behind Javier and embraced him with clear intent. Javier laughed and paused long enough for Gabriel to enter him. Javier gasped, but then laughed even louder as the three of us made a luscious, undulating sandwich. It was as if Gabriel were fucking me, but through a proxy. The weight of the two of them on my body was wonderful. The warmth of our three bodies together was reassuring. I loved that Gabriel was so close to me I could grab him with my hands. And yet when I pulled him closer to me, there was another hot body separating us—another delicious male body was between us, eager to be savored. It was strange, but I was all in. I was good for the long haul.

Our play lasted as long as these things can, which is never long enough, unfortunately. But when we finished, we were all three of us laughing, and rolling around on that nice big bed. We kissed some more, and then it was over. "Now I really have to take a shower!" Javier said. I rose and went to the linen closet to get him a towel. I watched him walk to the bathroom and thought, *What a beautiful body! And a sweetheart, too. We're lucky this turned out as well as it did. We might have ended up in bed with a psycho.*

"What do you think?" I asked Gabriel while Javier was showering.

"It was fun. What do you think?" he asked.

"I also thought it was fun. Great fun. But would you mind terribly if we never do this again?" I asked.

"Of course not. You know how I feel. That hasn't changed. Come here, Kitten," Gabriel said. I moved to him and he wrapped his arms around me and kissed me. "I love you. You're all I want."

"Smart man," I said. "I'll just go and see if our guest needs anything." The water had stopped. I tapped on the bathroom door. Javier opened it and smiled at me as he stood there in all his tan beauty. This was really the first time I got a complete look at the body I had just enjoyed. And it was stunning. "Do you need anything?" I asked.

"I already got all I needed," he said, as he finished drying himself. His dick said he was good for another round. And mine started to give me away as well. I could have sunk to my knees and taken him into my mouth. Maybe the whole thing. Or most of it anyway. I like to take dick down my throat. And I'm pretty good at it, if I do say so myself.

But instead, I simply said, "Thank you, Javier."

"Thank *you*," he said. "That was fun. You two are hot. I'm glad we did that."

"So am I," I said. "Very glad. But do you mind if we don't do it again?"

"Of course not," he said. "You two have a life that doesn't include me. I know that. But thanks for the invitation. I wouldn't have missed if."

Some situations turn out well, in life. This was one of them: Gabriel and I renewed our vow of fidelity. And we also made a new friend—a very nice young man who would always share with us a special bond of experience. There are different kinds of intimacy, I think. And one of those we would share with Javier for the rest of our lives.

Chapter Eight

By 1975, I was established enough at the Met that I heard René Claireau was looking for a new assistant. It would be a wonderful opportunity for Gabriel. It would get him to Paris. Claireau knew everybody. It was maybe the best thing that could happen to Gabriel just at that point in his career. A chance to meet people. A chance to have his own work seen by important gallerists.

And I had to decide whether or not to tell him about it. I only hesitated for only a few minutes—well, maybe for a day. I couldn't deny him the chance. Because I adore him. And I want only the best for him. The fact that I also wanted him to turn down the opportunity because he couldn't bear the thought of being parted from me was another issue entirely.

There was an interview process, of course. The fact that Gabriel was a known quantity at the Met did no harm. The chief curator for the Modern department gave his blessing. And then they flew him to Paris to meet Claireau himself in his studio. Gabriel was long on charm—and substance, too. And so when he got the job, I was not surprised. He was radiant, of course, when he flew home to wrap up his affairs in New York.

"It's like a dream," Gabriel said. "Paris? René Claireau? And I owe it all to my Kitten."

"It's only what you deserve, Gabe," I said. Of course I also believed he deserved *me*, first and foremost. But that was beside the point. "What is this going to look like?" I asked.

"What do you mean, darling?" he asked.

"You're leaving me, Gabe. I need to know the terms."

"I could never leave you. You know better than that."

"I know what I see," I said, "and I see you walking out the door in three days and taking a flight to Paris and not coming back for at least a few years, if at all. That's what I see."

"It's not like that, Kitten," Gabriel said. "We have to be apart for a bit. I don't know how long. But there are flights and telephones and post offices, and we'll get through this, just as we always have."

"I'm not certain I can live without you, Gabe," I said.

"Kit, you can do anything. But you don't have to live without me, you just have to let me go. For now."

"I want what's best for you," I said.

"And I want what's best for *you*. Speaking of which: We're young. People have needs. I don't expect you to be a hermit while I'm away."

"So you think I should have affairs?" I asked, dramatically.

"No. I think you should live your life. And I'm not expecting to come home to a saint. Please don't make this more difficult than it has to be, Kitten. You know what I'm saying," he said. And, of course, I did know what he was saying. I just didn't want to hear it. We had never been apart for more than a few days in the last five years. And in all that time we had never had sex with other men (except for Javier, of course, but that was different). I certainly had not had sex with another man. And I was certain that Gabriel had not either. And now the separation seemed so unlikely and sad.

"Angel, I want you to live this experience to the fullest. I want you to turn Paris on its ear. And if you end up in strange beds, then so be it. But, please, promise you'll never tell me." Gabriel reached out and held me. It was all said, but still the next two days were grim for me. I was devastated by the prospect of being alone, after five years of sharing my life with my perfect mate.

In a rational moment, I realized I only had two choices: I could accept Gabe's terms—a necessary but temporary separation. Or I could tell him never to return and slam the door on him when he left for Kennedy Airport. I've worked up some drama a time or two in my life, but the latter choice was not an option. I hunkered down and tried to stomach the concept of living alone.

For the first few months I felt like a monk. I worked five days a week and then went to the Y to swim. And that was about it. I didn't even pay attention to the hot guys in the locker room. Well, hardly ever. I whacked-off now and then to make sure I could. But there was no joy in it. Weekends I mostly spent reading and studying the catalogs of great painters.

My diet suffered from a lack of interest and I started to lose weight. And there was no weight to lose safely. I knew I was losing strength, too. I began to feel it in the swimming pool. It worried me, of course. Swimming was the only passion I had left, and if I lost that then I might as well lie down and die. But I couldn't figure out how to climb out of my slump.

That winter Karl spent most of February in town. He wasn't due back until spring, and yet, there he was. Upstairs, in our old apartment. Karl said he had some business to complete. I never questioned it. I love the city in all seasons, and so does he. I saw him one morning in the hall on my way to work, and he said, "Let me take you to dinner tonight. You look as if you could use a good meal."

I said, "Thanks, Karl, but I want you to come to me." He agreed, reluctantly. I'm not much of a cook, but I do know how to host. Southern boys have genetic coding for that. I fluffed, and polished, and tried to make everything inviting. As much as Gabriel and I had made that apartment our home, it was still Karl's. And I wanted him to be proud of how we occupied it. I had some cooked dishes I bought at Balducci's, and some other things I cobbled together on my own. I'm not stupid. I can get some food on the table and make it look inviting at the same time.

Karl arrived with a bottle of wine and a little bouquet of flowers that seemed impossibly springlike while there was still snow just outside the garden door. Karl, of course, knew where to find the perfect vase for the flowers. And we put them on the dining table. "I could teach you to cook," Karl said, "but then you might want to teach me to swim, and well, that ship has sailed. I suspect you're just perfect with your current skill set."

"Karl, I'm so delighted to see you," I said. "The last few months have been crazy with Gabriel away."

"I've been worried about you."

"That's very kind, but I'm fine, as you see," I said.

"What I see is that you look like shit. I know how Kit looks. And this isn't you."

"Thank you, Karl, but who are you, my Fairy God-father?"

"Yes, and you've always known that. So don't fuck with me. Just let me help you," he said.

"I don't need your help, again," I said.

"You need exactly what I'm about to tell you. But first, let's cut through the bullshit. You know I love you. Both of you. Since the morning you two showed up on my doorstep. Fugitives from the South. Gabriel could have been my Johnny, and you could have been me. Or you could have been the son I never had. And you think I'm going to just ignore you now? Kit, you have to embrace life. You have to eat, and drink, and suck all the juices out of every day. Work and swimming? Both good. Not enough! Take it all! You know how. It's who you are. You've just forgotten. It'll come back to you as soon as you try. Gabriel needs your strong and wonderful self as much as you do. We all do. We all need your best self."

"Karl, I just don't feel it anymore," I said.

"Kit, if I didn't love you, I'd give up on you. Self-pity is like a hog wallow. I thought I'd couch that in terms a Southern boy can understand. Look. Kit, you're so young and beautiful that you owe life your best shot. You owe it to those who love you. I'll be in town for another week. If you don't bound up the stairs and rap on my door in the next few days to tell me about some hot guy you've just fucked, then I'll give up on you. I swear I will. It will break my heart, but I'll do it."

"What if *he* fucks *me*? Does that count?" I asked.

"Depends on his dick size. And whether or not I get to watch."

"Karl, couldn't we lose the middle man? Couldn't we make love, you and I, right here on the dining table, right now?" I was only half joking. I would gladly have made love to Karl and considered it an honor.

"Kit Prescott, I do declare you've come back to life. And about your question: There's nothing that would give me greater joy than to make love to you. Nothing. But it's not going to happen. I'm not your answer. I'm your godfather, remember?"

After work and the pool, a few days later, I stopped off at a neighborhood bar—of which there were many—and ordered a beer. I helped myself to peanuts. There was a guy down the bar I'd seen before. We had smiled at each other when passing on the sidewalk. He came over and introduced himself: "Ronnie."

"Kit."

"A pleasure," we said in unison. Ronnie was a hot guy, Italian-looking, maybe; smallish, but with a huge bulge in his jeans.

"You live on Bank Street, don't you?" he asked.

"Guilty as charged," I said.

"I live right around the corner, and I'd really like you in my bed. What do you say?"

"I say, yes," I said. We left together, and within what seemed like seconds we were naked and in Ronnie's bed. What a romp! The memory of it still makes me smile. It was like trying to screw a roller-coaster. It was all-over-the-place, and juicy, and just plain carnal. It was a welcome change, after the somberness of the last few months.

It wasn't late when I got home, so I walked up to Karl's door and tapped very lightly. He answered and ushered me in, indicating the foot of his bed for me to sit. Karl was wearing a robe, and he was obviously bedded down for the night with a book. He settled back into bed and adopted a parental tone. "And where have you been, young man?" he asked.

"In a wanton embrace," I answered."

"As if you had to tell me. I can smell sex at fifty paces. It always was my favorite scent. Was it good?"

"It was—interesting," I said. "How much detail would you like?"

"You can skip the foreplay and get right to the fucking."

"That's what *we* did, too," I said. "It was a neighborhood guy named Ronnie."

"Nice ass."

"So you know him!"

"I know everybody," Karl said.

"Well, this guy wanted me up his—very nice—ass really badly. I always try to be careful. I mean, I don't want to hurt anybody. Well this guy wanted it rough. 'Harder, harder!' Like that. I did my best to provide the ride he wanted. I can't say he got it, but when he came he splashed all over his face, and my face, and our chests, and the bed. There was cum everywhere. And we both started to laugh. It's been a long time since I had such fun." I grew silent.

"My work here is finished," Karl said. "Good timing. I'm headed back to Connecticut on Thursday. Kiss your godfather good night."

And I did. Obediently. As always.

.

Chapter Nine

I started to focus on eating properly. I began to eat eggs for breakfast. Even when I stopped at a coffee shop after work, I made it a point to order meat and vegetables. Mostly every weekend I would pan-grill a big steak and devour it along with a big salad filled with good fresh veggies. Within a few months I had my muscle tone back. And my coloring improved. One morning I happened to catch a glimpse of myself in the mirror. It made me stop and study. _Kit, you're lookin' good_, I said to myself. And so I was.

It was in late spring the Met hired a new kid—from Atlanta—to work in the Greek & Roman department. Jeremy was a cute little thing with a terrific smile. He started flirting with me. And to my surprise, I liked it. We were having coffee together one afternoon on our breaks when I asked him, "Jeremy, do you think of yourself as more Greek or Roman?"

"I think I'm whatever the situation requires," he said.

"Good man!" I said. "Do you think you could join me for a Greek—or Roman—dinner some evening this week?"

"I'd be delighted," he said. "Choose a day."

"Friday?"

"Perfect."

"Greek?"

"Perfect."

"There's a little neighborhood restaurant near my apartment you might like," I said.

"I'm sure I will," he said.

"Then why don't we meet at the exit at the end of the day, and just go there together?"

"Sounds great," Jeremy said. "I'm looking forward."

"And so am I," I said. I hadn't really flirted in years, and then I suddenly felt my sap rising again, as if after a long cold winter. Spring was working its magic, inside and out.

Jeremy and I shared a good dinner, and a good visit, and a carafe of decent retsina. It felt good to participate in life a bit, to share a meal with a fellow human again. We laughed easily and flirted openly and naturally. "Will you come to my apartment?" I asked.

"I'd like that," he said. No surprise there. I expected he would. I let us in and put on a few lights. And then it was Jeremy who came to me with a kiss. I returned it. It felt good. It felt right. I led him to the bedroom.

We stripped and started to figure each other out. It had been unusually hot recently, and it was the end of a work day. I liked the slightly salty taste of Jeremy's skin. I found that I liked really everything about him. I wanted to enjoy him, but I also wanted to please him. I wanted to be a good lover. I wanted to be gentle and bold and masterful. I hadn't been held tenderly in such a long time that I was moved to tears. When we embraced our bodies had a natural fit.

Jeremy drew me close to him, and yet he yielded to my every move, to each caress, as if we were actually lovers. *Real* lovers. I began to explore his body as if the male form were new terrain. I almost wished that we had showered before falling into bed together. Because then I could have buried my face in his armpits without the metallic tang of chemicals. *Another time*, I thought. He was otherwise perfect just as he was at that moment. Jeremy's dick was generous and ramrod-straight, with an endearing freckle near the head. And his nipples were full and pink and begging to be nibbled.

As I continued my explorations, I discovered that Jeremy had a really beautiful ass. Anything that perfectly formed is difficult to hide, of course, so I knew it was there. I just didn't know that I would be overcome by it. But I was. I eased Jeremy's legs toward his torso, and he held them in his hands while I went for the sweet spot. I had nearly forgotten how wonderful men's bodies are. I had nearly forgotten the sweet taste of sweat on a man's chest, on his stomach, on his back, on his balls, on his asshole. But Jeremy refreshed my memory. I stayed down there as long as I dared. I was hungry for it. God knows how long I might have stayed if Jeremy hadn't said, "Please, Kit. I want you inside."

It was just the spur I needed. I rose from my obsessive devotion and took charge. I put Jeremy's slim young legs over my shoulders and mounted him. He was ready. He took it. I was just as gentle as I could manage to be, but Jeremy seemed ready to accept whatever I could offer. Big dick is the most important part of that equation. I have that. Not like Gabriel, of course. But why am I saying that? Why does everything come back to Gabriel?

You know how some people have a sex face that's a little scary? Not Jeremy. As we engaged, he began to look positively angelic. Like a choirboy. I wanted him, he wanted me, and we held each other as tightly as we dared. It was a lovely dance. Is that all it was? I can tell you that after a good, long, unhurried time in that embrace, I managed that old male cliché, "I'm going to come." And Jeremy's very nice dick with the freckle on it—with no other stimulation than what I provided him from within—began to spurt great waves of jism. *Matching mine*, I thought. *I did that, I thought. I made him come with me. Because he wanted me so much.*

Did I get a little weepy? Of course. We enjoyed the afterglow without any hurry. But then it was time to say good night. Did I invite Jeremy to sleep over? No. I had never shared that bed with any man other than Gabriel. Not on my own, at least. A sleepover felt much too intimate. I just couldn't do it. "When can I see you again?" Jeremy asked.

"Other than every day at work?" I asked.

"Other than every day at work," he said.

"Whenever you like," I said, and I meant it.

"Honest?" he asked.

"Honest," I answered.

"Good. I'll hold you to it," Jeremy said. And then we shared a kiss.

A wave of sweetness flowed over me as the nice young man bade me good night and slipped away into the darkness. I poured myself a glass of wine and neatened up the apartment a bit. Jeremy made me smile, for the first time, really, in nearly six months. *Am I actually getting my life back?* I wondered. *Surely I used to love to laugh, and play, and fuck as much as any man. I could be that Kit again, couldn't I?*

But then I started to weep. *Fuck you, Gabriel,* I thought. *How dare you do this to me! You won't hold me, and you won't release me. And I'm just stuck in the middle. And here's this perfectly nice kid with a lovely little body and a great dick. He deserves attention. He deserves a man of his own. And I can't be that man, because I'm your man. And you're in Paris. And fuck you very much!*

I cried myself to sleep that night. And a few others that week. But I also made date with Jeremy for a little supper on Wednesday, and a real dinner and whatever might happen afterward on Friday. I simply decided to enjoy the relationship. Wherever it might lead. Did I want to convince Gabriel I could be just fine without him? Maybe, but there didn't seem much chance of convincing myself.

I saw Jeremy often at work, of course. We had coffee a few times a week, and we scheduled occasional dinners and more proper dates mostly on Fridays, when we knew we could sleep late the next morning. It was great fun, and the sex was always exceptionally good. A few dates in, Jeremy rolled me over on my belly and began to explore my ass. He took to it just as fervently as I to his. And after a while he asked, timidly, "Kit, may I?"

"Yes, please," I answered. He changed his position so as to top me with the full weight of his little frame. It felt warm and reassuring. I hadn't felt pressure like that in longer than I dared remember. I welcomed Jeremy's nice hard dick inside me. I gave him my body to use as he saw fit. It was only half mine. The rest was Gabriel's, of course, but I gave my half to Jeremy. He took it. He explored my interior as carefully as any good prospector would. And he embraced my arms and shoulders and kissed my face. It was lovely.

When Jeremy came inside me I slipped into a sort of Zen zone that was very like napping. And when I returned to my senses, he was still inside. And then he stirred to life himself and began to move gently. This time I went beyond mere surrender to a more active giving. I met each thrust eagerly. He held my head and I met his mouth with mine. I gave everything I could with a purpose: I wanted to please. I wanted to be the perfect vessel.

How long was Jeremy inside me? I have no idea. Love-making happens on a different timetable than other activities, I always thought. I was good for the duration. I was ready for the whole night. But of course, these things can't last forever. People have to get up to pee. The spell is broken. As Jeremy began to dress, I said, "Will you stay over?"

"I'd love to, Kit, but I have a really early morning. I hope you'll ask me again some time."

"Of course," I said. One more kiss, and he was gone.

It was probably the next Friday night—when we knew we'd have some real time to spend together—

that we met for dinner and then came back to the apartment. Jeremy was just as sweet as before. When I reached for him, he came to me. And when I kissed him, he kissed me back with passion. But when I started to undress him, Jeremy said, "Kit, we need to talk."

"Of course," I said, "but couldn't it wait until after we make love?"

"No, I think it has to be now," Jeremy said.

"Yes, if you say so." There was a leaden feeling in my belly. But what could I do?

"At first I wanted your body," Jeremy said. "And Kit, I have to tell you it's beyond my expectations. And the more I see your body, and the more I touch you, the more beautiful it becomes. Then I wanted your friendship, which you gave me."

"Yes, I did."

"But soon I wanted more: I wanted *you*. And that I can't have. I'm in love with you, Kit, and you'll never love me back. I can't do it anymore. I can't see you. It's not enough. We both deserve better."

I reached for Jeremy and he fell into my arms, as eagerly as ever. I kissed him, and then kissed him some more. "Jeremy, will you sleep over tonight?" I asked.

"Yes, Kit, thank you. I hoped you'd ask. And then when I leave in the morning, it's over."

I gulped at the finality of it all. "Then we'd better make the most of tonight," I said.

"Yes, please." This time we started in the shower. When we fell into bed together, I was more than ready to enjoy every sweet inch of Jeremy's body with no interference from Proctor & Gamble. His armpits were even more exciting than I imagined—sweet, masculine, seductive. I tried my best to give his whole body equal attention. But I kept dividing my focus between Jeremy's beautiful ass and his luscious mouth. We kissed so deeply we seemed to blend into one being. I was precisely where I wanted to be.

And we got down to serious love-making. The fact of its being the last time made it feel more urgent than ever. And yet I forced myself to slow down. Jeremy seemed to be memorizing each curve of my body. I approached his body the same way. Those precious memories would have to be enough. "I love you, Kit," Jeremy said.

"And I love you. I do, Jeremy. It's just that I gave my heart away years ago, and now there's nothing much left to give."

"Thank you for your honesty. And when I get over you, I think I'll look back on this as the happiest time of my life. Do we have to go to sleep? Couldn't we just hold each other until dawn?"

"I'd like that," I said. And so we did. We sat together—arms and legs entwined—and cradled each other for hours. We also shared one last orgasm, blending our essences and marking both our bodies with the combination.

When the first light of dawn shown softly through the edges of the window shades, Jeremy roused himself and said, "I'll go now."

"I'll make coffee," I said.

"No, Kit. I can't bear to draw this out any longer. And besides, there'll be plenty of time for coffee in the future. And while we're sharing it, I'll say to myself, 'This beautiful man once gave me every ounce of himself he could.' That's the truth, isn't it?"

"Yes, the truth," I said. Jeremy started to weep softly, and that set me off, too. But we were both wrung out, so it didn't last long. Jeremy rose and dressed, and then he was gone. I was suddenly exhausted and threw myself back into bed. The sheets were still warm, and they still smelled of Jeremy. I conked out instantly and slept deeply for several hours.

When I woke I was hungry, of course. After an egg and a bite of cheese, I headed out to the Y for a swim. It always clears my head and helps me get my bearings. I did laps for about a half hour, easily, at a measured pace. And then I dressed and walked home.

After opening some blinds I fluffed sofa pillows and organized the living room. Then I changed the bed. Did I hold the old sheets to my nostrils and hope to inhale Jeremy's scent? Only once. Just as a reality check, I told myself. And then I headed to the kitchen to make coffee. Once I was seated at the breakfast table with a steaming mug of coffee and hot milk in front of me, I got out pen and paper and started a letter to Gabriel:

How is my Angel?

I hope Paris is treating you well. Or perhaps I hope Paris is treating you so badly you'll come right home. Both, I guess. I wish I could send you some exciting news from New York, but the Met is the same, and the McBurney pool is the same. And that's really the scope of my existence.

Could we meet? Here? There? Bermuda is just about in the middle. How about Bermuda? I don't care. I just need my Angel. This separation is dangling me between worlds, and I doubt I have the strength for it.

As always, I want only what's best for you. But then I always thought that what's best for you is me. Just give me a weekend. Or something. Something to remind me why I gave you my whole heart. And why I've never wanted it back.

Your Kitten

Chapter Ten

We did meet in Bermuda. And not a moment too soon, as far as I was concerned. The hotel was luxurious and the pink-sand beaches lovely. But it was only Gabriel that interested me. We never left the hotel room, spending nearly every moment in bed. Mostly we got up for an occasional room-service meal, then tumbled back into bed. The maid brought us fresh towels. We had everything we needed.

"Tell me about Paris," I said over breakfast on Sunday morning. In a few hours I'd be on my way to the airport. The time had passed so quickly.

"Claireau is demanding," he said, "and often unpleasant. But he's an amazing painter. Some of his new work is remarkable. Maybe some of his best. And some of it's . . . disappointing. The interesting thing for me is that he knows when it's right and when it isn't. And he keeps on working no matter what. I admire that."

"It really is where you need to be, isn't it," I said.

"I'd be home in a heartbeat, otherwise," Gabriel said, "home to my Kitten. And how are you?

I didn't have an answer. Or not one that didn't sound selfish to me. "I'm proud of you," I said. And then I started to cry. Gabriel dashed over and grabbed me. He pushed the room-service table aside and sank to his knees between mine. He dropped his hotel robe and pushed mine open so that nothing could come between us. He buried his face in my lap and shed a few tears of his own. I held his head as tenderly as if it were my newborn. And I remembered the first time we made love. And the next. And the next.

It wasn't enough—having Gabriel for only a weekend. But it was something; something to fill the void while he was in Paris. I didn't see him again for several months, not until the Met sent me to London as front-man for a Sargent show coming up the next year. I phoned Gabriel to ask him to meet me, and to my great relief, he said, "Of course." There were loans to arrange. The Tate had some lovely Sargents, including the wonderful full-sized sketch for Madame X. I was thrilled at the thought of comparing the sketch and the finished canvas side by side. And that was exactly what we had in mind for the big show coming up. Could I get it? If anyone could, I could—not because I was such a persuasive negotiator, but because I represented the Metropolitan Museum of Art.

There were many other Sargents in London, of course. Some grand and some small and charming. It was my job to see what I could secure for our show—what we could borrow to fill the gaps in our own coverage. We were short on watercolors, for instance, while several small collections in London were rich in them. Like that. There would be a wonderful mix.   One of my colleagues had already managed to convince the Freer in DC to lend *Break-fast in the Loggia*. It was the first painting I really fell in love with, and the thought of having it on view at the Met—in my own back yard—was thrilling. And speaking of DC, the National Gallery would most likely be good for a few important loans. We were rivals, but we also knew we had to be generous with each other.

For the London trip, the Met put me up at the Ritz. That kind of extravagance was not their style at all, but the galleries in London had connections and special rates, so it was all arranged. And Picca-dilly was a convenient, central location. I set out to ask for all the works we most wanted to borrow, and to my great relief, I got a conditional "yes" for nearly all of them. Even the *Madame X* sketch at the Tate. Much would depend upon what the Met would be willing to lend in future. But that was out of my hands. My work was done.

Gabriel got in that Friday evening—after a bumpy Channel crossing. We had dinner in the rococo splendor of the Ritz dining room. The food was not great, but it was skillfully prepared. I knew it would fortify us for the reunion to come. Just like our Ber-muda visit, we took to our bed and hunkered down. The next morning, we ordered a room service break-fast and lay in bed, holding each other, until it arrived. While pouring coffee, I said, "Angel, this separation is killing me."

"Well, you'll certainly leave a pretty corpse, Kit-ten," he said.

"Gabe, I'm hurting over here. How can you be flip with me?"

He reached for my hand. "Forgive me. It's painful for me, too. In case you haven't noticed. I think of you all day—while I'm running errands for Claireau, while I'm stretching new canvases for him and setting them up. While I'm painting. Especially while I'm painting. Every brush stroke is for you. I can't even mix a color without feeling you behind me, approving. Or disapproving. It's all about you, Kitten. And at night . . . ."

"I swore I wouldn't ask, but I can't help myself. How much longer?"

"I wish I knew. I can't even say how long Claireau will want me there. A year? Maybe two? But it can't be like this. We have to see each other at least every two or three months. We'll just do it. You'll come to Paris. You have vacation time due. I'll go to New York. I can always get away for a few days. We'll make it work."

"A few days every few months. I don't know. It still feels like torture. I'd almost rather . . ."

"Don't say it!"

"Give you up. There, I said it."

"Please don't talk that way again," Gabriel said. "It's too painful."

"Tell me! Angel, I'm flying home tomorrow, and you're going back to your new home . . ."

"Temporary home!"

"Temporary home, then," I said. "And I don't have the will to fight. I'll do it your way. Phone me, or write me, and tell me when we can meet again. And I'll show up. Let's not talk about this anymore. Let's enjoy the few precious moments we have together." And we did.

Every two or three months. I was resigned. I hated it, but it was our reality. And in between, how about the Jeremys of life? Were there others? No. Impossible. The emotional wear-and-tear is too great. I refused to go there ever again. What about sex? Yes. I could find sex on any street in Manhattan. I could have put on a three-piece suit and gone down to Wall Street for sex. I didn't—not that uptight young brokers didn't interest me—but I could have made the trip and been fucking in a corporate men's room by lunchtime. But I had a job. So instead, I found comfort after hours with Met colleagues and neighborhood guys. Whenever I needed it. There were hot guys from the gym—*in* the gym, even. I took whatever my body needed. I gave only what my body could share.

When a nice guy I met in a bar asked me home, I usually went. I jumped in with abandon and celebrated life and lust. My body was largely present. If some guy needed me to fill him, I filled him. If some guy needed to fill me, I surrendered. If some guy needed to be held, I held him. And if some guy needed to hold me, I let him.

I'll take a big dick any day. I'll take a small dick any day—they're easier to suck. Cut? Sure. Uncut? Even better. But it's all in the man rather than the dick. Balls? Yes, please. Two, if possible. One will do nicely. Large and low if I can get them. Or however they're made. All balls are good. I'll take any reasonably nice-looking man as long as he smells good and doesn't seem to inspire ominous foreboding. Boys don't interest me anymore, but older men can be exceptionally hot.

Occasionally I headed out to a bathhouse. There were at least a half dozen well-known, popular ones in those days, in Manhattan alone. I loved the furtiveness, the low lighting, the steam and sauna and shower. I would happily lie down in the middle of the orgy table and wait for a group scene to develop. And it never took long for one to develop. I never said no to any guy who wanted to join in. After all, what's the point of group sex with discrimination? No. When I made my body available, I made it available to any man who wanted it. And, fortunately, many men did want it. I took. I gave. If they wanted tender, I was tender. If they wanted rough, I did my best at rough. If they wanted to sit on my face, I accepted them. If they wanted *me* to sit on *their* faces, I obliged.

If a dozen men lined up waiting for the chance to fuck me, I tried to accommodate them all, to the best of my ability. And one night when a sweet-faced young guy was in that same posture, I got in line and waited my turn. I gave him my best shot, saying to myself, *This is for you, Jeremy. This is for the love that couldn't be. This is for us.* And when I came inside that kid, did I believe I had made love to Jeremy? Of course not. But I needed the fantasy just the same. And he needed what I could offer. I felt a moment of exquisite tenderness as I erupted inside that guy. And I fancied that he looked up from all the other dicks—in his hands and in his mouth—and looked me squarely in the eyes with a gesture of gratitude.

I didn't want to pull out. He didn't want me to leave, even though there were others waiting to service him. "Thank you," he said softly. I'm sure he did. Well, I might be wrong. But it was over. Before I left the orgy room, when the next man had already started in on my new little friend's ass, I stopped to kneel by his face. The man whose dick was filling his mouth backed away politely while I kissed the kid deeply. He responded in kind.

"Be safe," I said.

"Thank you, Sir Galahad," he said. And I moved aside, politely, and surrendered the territory to the big dick that had been there before. I stepped back and watched for a while. As scenes go, this was hot stuff. I even considered getting back in line for another chance. But really, how stupid is that? Did the guy really remind me of Jeremy, or of myself? Hard to say.

There were so many visits to the baths and so many scenes that most of it's awash in my memory. But whatever happened—in the orgy room or the private rooms or the steam room or the sauna, for that matter—when I was sated, I showered one last time and headed home. And I always felt as if I had been washed clean. As if I had just come from a revival meeting. As if I had been saved.

Did I go to the S & M bars in the Meatpacking District? Mostly as a tourist. And only a few times. I liked the smell of it. I liked the camaraderie. I always thought leather men are the sweetest men I've known. The sense of trust is palpable. I wanted that community. But role-playing and delivering—or receiving—pain just didn't work for me. I took the kiss of the lash on my bare back once. I understood that it was a caress from the hot guy who delivered it. I accepted it. Did I even come while being flogged (ever so gently, of course.)? Maybe. I still have the vest, the harness, and the chaps I bought at the Leather-Man. Nothing would induce me to part with them. It was great fun, but it wasn't quite me.

I never brought another man home to my bed—Gabriel's and my bed. That I couldn't do. And Gabriel? How did he satisfy his needs while he was in Paris? We kept to our bargain. Neither of us ever broached the subject of other men. It was unacceptable. It was not part of our agreement. It was not part of the life we shared. It had nothing to do with our love. It was irrelevant, really. And it was the past.

Chapter Eleven

It wasn't until the spring of 1980 that Gabriel finally came home to me. We were only thirty, so we still felt like kids. Gabriel had grown even more handsome while he was away. And even, well, a little Parisian, I guess. He wore clothes better than ever. And he gained a new confidence about life and his work. I saw it immediately. And when we were out-and-about in the neighborhood, I saw it in the faces of the people we passed. He was stunning. He was home. And he was mine. And if we were together and happened to run into some neighborhood guy I had a fling with in the years before, then we stopped for introductions and a quick kiss. And then Gabriel and I continued on our way.

Gabriel rented studio space that first month. He needed it. He had started to paint in rather large format. I hadn't seen much of the new work, and it would take another month or more for the cargo container to ship to New York. He needed space and light, and he got it, a little farther downtown. Tribeca was the new name for that old industrial neighborhood. The loft he found could have been converted to include residential space. We spoke of it, of course. But neither of us was willing to give up Bank Street. It was our haven eight years before, and it remained exactly that.

Gabriel fell into a new routine right away, rising early and heading to the studio to paint. I was so proud of his focus. While he was living in Paris, he developed an exercise program that was mostly plyometrics, I think. The new studio gave him plenty of room for lunges and squats and planks. And he walked to work and back most days. So he stayed fit. And by the time I got home from work at the Met—and my obligatory after-work swim at the Y— Gabriel was home and ready to play.

And play we did. As if making up for lost time, we went out to dinner nearly every evening that first year he was back. And we made love. We made love whenever possible. Often at night, at bedtime. Sometimes on Saturday morning or Sunday after-noon. Every time he kissed me I wanted more. There was not one moment in that decade that I didn't want him. That I didn't want to be his. That I didn't want to hold him until we fell asleep at night.

The first time I wanted to top Gabriel, he seemed surprised. As if his kitten should be just shy and retiring. He knew better, of course. He knew every-thing. He understood exactly what Karl had been trying to tell me. Gabriel knew I launched his career. He had keen insight—clearer than mine—into what it takes to make things work in the real world. We didn't always verbalize these things, but we knew. We both knew. And yet we never really discussed it at all until the night that I wanted with all my heart to be inside my precious mate.

"Angel," I said, "please let me in."

"Kitten, have I ever denied you anything? Have I ever said no to anything you wanted?"

"Never. And now there's something I need to know. There's something you have to tell me. I'll wait. I'll wait a lifetime. But you have to tell me. That is not negotiable."

"I know, Kitten," he said. "I should have told you ten years ago. But I didn't. And I hoped I'd never have to."

"This is your story, Angel, not mine. It's up to you."

"When I was ten . . ."

"Oh, shit! Don't go there if you don't want to."

"No, you're right, Kitten. I can't run away from this any longer. When I was ten, I was walking home from school one evening. I was there late finishing a picture for the art show coming up the next week. I was only a few blocks from home when a car started bearing down on me. I had to dive into the ditch to avoid being hit. The car pulled over—I'll never forget it was a '57 Chevy, gray and green. Out came four teen-aged white boys who had obviously been drinking. I started to run, but there were four of them, so they caught me easily.

" 'You're a pretty little nigger, ain't ya,' one of them said. And the others joined in with catcalls and jeers. They dragged me to the car and stuffed me in the back seat between two of them. The other two got into the front seat and the car sped off. 'What do you think, boys?' the driver asked. 'Should we have some fun with our new little friend?' They all agreed, 'yes,' and off we went to a dirt road on the edge of town. And you know Claysville has plenty of dirt roads. Did then, anyway."

Gabriel fell silent for a moment. I could see the pain in his eyes. I wanted to hold him, but I also wanted him to finish telling his story out loud. "They pulled over and we all got out. The driver was obviously the ringleader of the group. Whatever he proposed, the others jumped right in. When they bent me over the hood of that '57 Chevy and pulled down my pants, it took all four of them to hold me down while the driver raped me. The other boys called out encouragement while he gave me thrust after thrust. There was lots of laughter. I never cried out. There was no one to hear me. And I knew the pain and the shame were mine alone.

"When the driver finished and one of the other boys took his place, I needed less restraint. I had lost the will to fight, and I just wanted it to be over. It wasn't, of course. Not for a while, anyway. Just when the third boy was finishing up, they spotted some headlights in the distance and scrambled to get themselves back into the car. The last one in pushed me into the ditch and they took off. They didn't even threaten me with violence if I told. There was no one to tell. They knew that. They were safe.

"I lay there for a few minutes trying to get my bearings. I didn't think I was going to die. I didn't even want to, really. I just didn't know how to go home and look as if nothing had happened. There would be no point in telling my parents. It would only upset them. And there was no justice. I came up with a plan:

"There was an old well on the side of the house. I pumped the handle and rinsed away the red clay dust from the road, and as much of the blood and cum as I could. When I walked in the kitchen door, I was pretty much myself. "Where have you been, child?' my mother demanded. I did my best imitation of cheerful as I told my mother the painting was go-ing really well (which was true) and that I had lost track of time and stayed too late. I told her:

" 'I think I got more paint on *me* than on the *paper,* so I thought I should rinse it off before I came in.'

" 'Get upstairs and get those wet clothes off,' she said. 'Put on something dry and get down here. I have some supper for you on the back of the stove. You know your daddy likes to eat on time. I stalled him for twenty minutes, but that was the limit. And bring me that wet mess, too. Gabriel Elijah, I swear you are more trouble than any two young'uns. If your brother and your sister turn out like you, I don't know what I'll do. Go on, now!'

"I did, of course. And I hoped that would be the end of it. I tried to check my ass, to see how much damage there was. The pain had started to lessen, and the bleeding had stopped. As far as I could tell. Seeing a doctor was really out of the question. This was my problem alone, and I would deal with it. The next afternoon when I walked home from school, Momma called me back to the kitchen, where she was doing laundry. "Gabriel, what is this?' she asked, indicating the traces of blood in my shorts that I had missed at the pump the night before.

" 'I can't tell you, Momma,' I said. She saw the resolve in my ten-year-old eyes and softened a bit.

" 'Come here, child,' she said and enveloped me in here arms. 'You can tell me anything. Always remember that.'

" 'I know, Momma. But not this.'

" 'Very well,' she said. 'It's your decision.'

" 'Thank you, Momma. And please don't worry Daddy with this. It'll only get him upset. And there's nothing to be done about it.'

" 'I think this could be our secret, whatever it is. If you change your mind, you can always come to me.'

" 'Thank you, Momma. I will.' Surely she knew something awful had happened. There was blood, and blood = violence. She probably guessed it. And no doubt she felt deep sadness that she was unable to keep her family safe. But she respected me, and we never spoke of it again. I never told anyone. And I hate that I never told you. It's part of who I am. You have a right to know."

"And now I do," I said. "I should have guessed there was something like that in your past. I did guess. I just didn't know what to ask. You never talk about your nightmares, so I can't know what they are, but I know when you're having them. Sometimes I have to restrain you when you start to thrash around. So you don't hurt yourself. Or me. I'm strong. I can take it." I wanted that to be the truth, for Gabriel's sake, and yet I had doubts about my own strength. Gabriel, on the other hand, was a tower of strength. Always had been. And there I was trying to offer him mine.

"I don't know why you love me," he said. "I'm a fucking mess."

"You're the most beautiful mess I ever clapped eyes on," I said. "Will you talk about your dreams?"

"They're not very original, I'm afraid: Klansmen in white robes; Claysville policemen running me in on made-up traffic charges; country boys with nooses. Like that."

"Thank you for telling me, Angel," I said. And I felt even closer to Gabriel. In fact, I felt we had washed ourselves clean of the past. It was like coming home from the baths. I had every answer I needed to my questions, except, "Will you let me inside you?"

"Yes. I've always wanted that. I've always wanted you to have me totally, just the way you've always given yourself to me. But not tonight, Kitten."

"I'm not a rapist," I said. "I'm not even much of a white boy anymore."

"You'll always be a white boy. But you're *my* white boy. Will you hold me until I fall asleep?"

"I'll hold you as long as you let me," I said.

We got into spoon formation. Always my favorite. I was exhausted. I think Gabriel was, too. When I woke the next morning I was still pressed against him, with my left arm still embracing his beautiful torso. As the first hint of consciousness came over me, it was Gabriel's breathing that caught my focus—his breathing and my morning wood pressed against him. And as much as I wanted to get up and go to the john to pee, I chose to lie perfectly still and listen to his breathing, and to feel his chest rise and fall. We touched in all the familiar places. I thought perhaps I knew his body better than my own. And yet every inch of it was as warm and new as if we had only just met. I began to weep softly. And then I was rescued from bed-wetting by the alarm clock.

Chapter Twelve

The decade of the 1980s seemed to speed by. I got some little promotions—and even smaller raises. The Met felt like a second home to me. It looked like I'd be there for the duration. Some other museums and even Christie's tried to lure me away with offers of higher salary and shorter hours. But making a change never felt like the right thing to do. No, I had found my niche.

Gabriel, too, found firmer footing. He all but stopped beating himself up about artistic choices that didn't pan out as he had hoped. He simply painted. Every weekday. And his work grew better and better. For a few years Gabriel painted a series of canvases that were dark and brooding. I wondered if he hadn't remembered, somehow, the Baskin prints we saw together on our first date. I never spoke of it. I always thought inspiration is a nonverbal phenomenon.

I can talk about pigments, colors, surfaces, and textures for days. But the finished work? It comes from a place of mystery and then exists in a new plane where it must speak for itself—where it speaks to the heart of each observer. I've written more than my share of explanatory text for wall plaques to accompany pictures in an exhibition. Trying to give viewers some context is what we do, after all. But I always try to avoid any reference to the meaning of a picture. And when I really have to pass along historical interpretations, then I always hope viewers will ignore pundit-speak and simply have their own conversation with the work.

When the Epidemic began to rear its ugly head in the early '80s, we watched it claim the lives of friends and colleagues. All around both of us. We didn't know any Haitians, or hemophiliacs, or intravenous drug users, or sex workers. But artists and other creatives? Many. We also didn't know many performers, but we read about them every morning in *The New York Times* obits. It was not only deeply disturbing but terrifying as well. Even when the particulars of HIV transmission became known, the past lingered with big question marks.

I never had sex with other men in the 1980s. And neither did Gabriel, as far as I know. That must have gone a long way toward keeping us safe. But really, how could we have dodged the bullet? Surely a plague of such virulence did not suddenly materialize one spring afternoon in 1981. No, it had roots. Deep roots, no doubt. And they surely reached back into the previous decade. I can't say how we avoided it. But we did.

Gabriel and I mostly drew in our family circle and focused on our lives and careers. We attended a lot of funerals and memorials, but then we returned home and redoubled our efforts to protect what was ours. Anti-gay sentiment ran so high in the right-wing population that it seemed to outstrip racism, for a change. It would have seemed a bizarre time to be alive had it not become merely quotidian.

We had dinner with friends. Often. Several women friends from the Met joined us now and then, especially a lesbian couple and a straight woman I worked with closely. Gabriel's new gallerist became a friend and dinner buddy. There were two gay (male) couples from the neighborhood whom Gabriel and I had known, and liked, for years. I suppose they, too, had been monogamous enough to escape the Epidemic. They had us over. We had them over. I never learned to cook, of course, but I faked it well.

Gabriel is not a committed cook, either. But he did learn, from his mother, how to fry chicken. And an aunt who grew up on the Chesapeake taught Gabriel to make delicious crab cakes and fried porgy (surely one of God's greatest creations). So he cooked for our guests now and then. And Gabriel also made spoon bread, and cheese grits, and a few egg dishes and other breakfasty things. So we occasionally had friends over for Sunday brunch. I would make a fruit salad and the mimosas. Brunch was always our most successful entertaining event. And we enjoyed it at least as much as our friends did.

I did most of the cleanup. I liked it, actually. Cleanup felt meditative. Not like swimming, exactly, but close. After all my childhood years of being waited on, I enjoyed pampering others and relieving Gabriel of any extra work. And our apartment— Karl's apartment—was so inviting and so well designed that it made a party seem effortless. We used it. We lived.

We kept in touch with Jerry Segal, the classmate in Chapel Hill who got the job at the Brooklyn Museum and who helped us figure out how to conquer

Greenwich Village. Jerry met the most delicious man—at the theater, as it happened, and not at a bar—and settled down. Jerry's partner, Rick, is an accountant. And a good one. We hired him immediately. Rick looks more like a porn star than a businessman, but he's quite solid. Gabriel and I bound our hearts to theirs. And Jerry and Rick are now family.

The event that really stands out from everything ordinary that decade was learning that Jeremy was sick. A colleague told me. I didn't want to believe it, but it was true. Jeremy and I had coffee one afternoon, as we had done so often through the years. He said, "Kit, I think you have a right to know I'm Positive."

"Thank you for telling me," I said, "but I already knew. And that's why I'm not getting crazy about it."

"Good," Jeremy said. "It doesn't help. Believe me."

"Jeremy," I said, "I know this is lame, but I want you to know how much I've valued our friendship all these years. And if there's anything I can do, just ask."

"Thanks, Kit. I will ask. But mostly I hope you'll continue to be my friend."

"That's a given," I said.

"Good. And now let's talk about something important, like improving the quality of the food in this cafeteria."

When Jeremy grew too weak to continue showing up for work, about six months later, I was horrified, of course. I developed the habit of stopping by his apartment after work, before heading to the Y for a swim. Sometimes I took him a flower, and sometimes some chocolates or a pastry. Other times I just showed up and sat with him for a while. And held his hand. It wasn't much, but it was what I had to offer. And he accepted it, just as he had always accepted me, limitations and all.

Gabriel never asked me for clarification. He simply adjusted to my new schedule. He knew. He must have known. And even when Jeremy died and I slipped into deep mourning, Gabriel never questioned my feelings. He attended the memorial with me. He was patient and supportive. And we both honored our truce with the past.

Momma and I talked on the phone once or twice a month. She usually called in the evenings, and I sometimes picked-up and sometimes left her call to the answering machine. I made it a point to phone the house every Wednesday afternoon, when I knew both Momma and Daddy would be out. That way I could talk freely with Esther and find out what was really going on in that household. If I had listened carefully to her in recent years, I wouldn't have been so shocked by Momma's call in 1990. It was just that Daddy had been a famous hypochondriac for decades. And so there was a trace of *The Boy Who Cried Wolf* in his story, as far as I was concerned.

Once Esther told me she was going to DC for a few days to visit her sister. Gabriel and I headed for Penn Station without a second thought and hopped on Amtrak. It was lovely to see Esther again. We shared a late breakfast and headed to the Freer, the three of us. And then we spent most of the afternoon at the National Gallery. We had dinner at Old Ebbitt

Grill and ate far too many oysters. It was a delightful day, but much too brief. When we found a cab and dropped Esther at her sister's house, the hugs were fierce. It was painful, parting with her again.

I never went to Claysville, of course, but Gabriel did. He went to see his family at least once a year, usually around Thanksgiving. Every year Gabriel's mother phoned me and invited me to come, too, to stay with the family. And every year I thanked her as warmly as I could and made excuses for why I couldn't make it. I simply couldn't do it. I couldn't bring myself to go back to that town. I sent holiday gifts to the Williamsons—replicas of the Met's Christmas tree ornaments, and snow globes, and other objects of wonder. I sent silk scarves and little silver gifts from Tiffany. I sent Gabriel's dad cigars from Nat Sherman. One year I sent a ham, without mentioning my plan to Gabriel. And then we both had a good laugh about my sending a ham to the heart of hog country.

I tried to get into the holiday spirit. I tried to be kinder to Momma. I sent her something every Christmas, even if it was only a little gold charm for her bracelet from the Met's gift shop. She didn't need anything, of course, except a reconciliation between Daddy and me. And that was the one gift I couldn't give. One year I sent Esther a string of pearls. I told her it was up to her whether she wanted to tell the church ladies they were real. She scolded me, when I spoke to her the Wednesday after Christmas. She said, "You know I don't believe in that kind of extravagance. I doubt I'll ever be able to wear them. But I'd certainly like to be buried in them, if you'd be so kind as to arrange it."

I'll always remember Gabriel's return from one of his family visits. Once we had unpacked his bags and enjoyed a good dinner, we were relaxing over dessert when Gabriel said. "I have to tell you, Kitten, these visits are not easy."

"Of course not, Angel," I said.

"But the odd part is this: You know I love my family. And when I'm with them I sometimes forget why I hate Claysville so much. But all it takes is one drive a little bit out of town and seeing the big billboard that announces THIS IS GOD'S COUNTRY. And then it all comes back to me: every hateful memory; all the fear; all the outrage."

I was willing to do without Gabriel for Thanksgiving as long as I could have him back for Christmas and New Year's. We spent them together, that decade. And we greeted each new year together with all the joy and optimism we could muster, which was considerable.

Chapter Thirteen

When Momma called that Monday morning to summon us to Claysville, one of my concerns—albeit a secondary one—was what to do with our new pet. The year before, Gabriel suggested getting a cat. But I was firm: "There's only room for one kitten in this household," I said. So instead we got a Jack Russell terrier puppy and named him Buster. Karl helped with the housebreaking, when he was in town. Karl had many dogs, through the years, and he was naturally affectionate as well as stern. Buster was rowdy, as all Jack Russels are, and all but untrainable. But Karl managed to set the minimum rules about walks and garden visits and acceptable behavior in the apartment in between. It worked.

I considered boarding Buster if we really had to travel. We had left him once or twice in a small kennel in the neighborhood. He seemed to be okay with it. But, luckily, Karl was in town and offered to house-sit with Buster while we were away. Things were falling into place. I called our travel agent and asked him to get round-trip tickets for us with open-ended returns.

Daddy's doctor was just on his way out the door when Gabriel and I arrived. "Hi, Dr. Simmons," I said. "Please meet my partner, Gabriel Williamson." After the how-do-you-dos were out of the way, the doctor said to me, quietly:

"Kit, your daddy's a very sick man. He's been carrying too much weight for decades; he only quit smoking last month; and he's been a heavy drinker all the years I've known him. Not a healthy combination. His heart is fragile. But he's a tough old bird, and he has no intention of leaving us until he settles some business with you. I hope you'll help him tell you what he needs to say, so he can find some peace."

"Of course, Dr. Simmons. Thank you. We'll see you . . .?"

"Tomorrow morning, most likely. But the nurse knows how to reach me just in case. I must go."

"Of course," I said. And he left the house. I turned to Gabriel with lots of questions in my eyes for which he had no more answers than I did.

Esther came down the stairs just at that moment and fell into my arms. She also embraced Gabriel. "Your old room is ready for you two. I don't think there's anyone to help with your bags just now, but you two look fit enough to handle them. Both of you. Yes. Very fit, indeed."

"Essie, I can't begin to tell you how much I've missed you," I said. "If only we could be meeting at a wedding, or something joyous. Anyway, please fill me in. I always feel like I get the truth from you."

"Kit, your momma is taking a nap, praise the Lord. She's been sleeping poorly for some time now. The doctor gave her something. And I wouldn't disturb her just now for the Second Coming. Why don't you two settle in—quietly—and then come down to see me?"

"Perfect," I said. I hated being back in that house, and yet it held so many lovely memories, too—Esther teaching me to write at the kitchen table; chasing my Easter ducklings on the back lawn; learning hand-stands and stilt-walking. I learned to swim in that pool, for fuck's sake. And—most precious of all—I remembered making tender love to Gabriel in my bed. We unpacked a little. I hung up my black suit. I told Gabriel he must not under any circumstances bring one. I told him that he would be in Claysville for two days, tops, and then back to reality. Back to finishing the most important collection of his career. Back where he belonged.

"Kit, you know your Daddy's health has been up and down for years," Esther told us when we met her in the kitchen. "I don't know exactly what Dr. Simmons told you: I always thought doctors have different stories for menfolk and womenfolk."

"I'm sure you're right," I said.

"But in this case I suspect I'm getting the straight talk, since he doesn't see me as someone whose delicate sensibilities need to be spared. Anyway, your daddy's dying, for sure. This time. But he won't go with you on his conscience. You do what you want, but I think the boy I raised will help his daddy find some peace at the end."

"Essie, you always did know exactly how to twist my ear. Look, I'm here. *We're* here. I'll do whatever's needed. I buried my hatchet so long ago I forget where it is." Was that the truth? Maybe. Largely. And yet just the fact of being in that house again set my teeth on edge.

"He's quiet at the moment, and he's usually at his best in the mornings. So I'm going to make a little supper for you boys and your momma, and then let's all get a good night's sleep."

Gabriel and I took a glass of wine out to the back patio and tried to enjoy the last of the daylight, to settle ourselves after our travel, and to process the situation. Little shimmers of sunset glanced off the surface of the pool. It could have been charming. But mostly I thought, *Claysville. Fuck! Here we are.* "Angel, I'm so sorry to do this to you!" I said.

"Shut up, Kitten!" he said. "I couldn't be any-where other than here with you."

"I wouldn't have dared to ask you to come if Momma hadn't insisted. I hoped it would be just my problem, alone. It *is* just my problem, alone. But there's some role for you, too. Whatever it is. And then we'll get you out of here as soon as possible."

"I didn't even tell my parents I'm in town," he said.

"Good!" I said. "You're not. This is an unofficial visit. It doesn't count."

Esther gave us supper. Momma seemed a bit frail—and old. But she was a Bullard, after all, and Bullards don't just fall apart when life hands them a challenge. No, I sensed she would come through this ordeal just fine. I also stopped worrying about how I would handle it. I would handle it. Simple.

"Thank you for coming, boys," Momma said.

"You don't need to thank us, Momma," I said. "Thank *you* for inviting us." She was playing her cards close to the vest. We still had no idea why Gabriel needed to be there.

"Kit's right, Miz Prescott," Gabriel said. "Thank you for the invitation."

"You could call me Vinni," Momma said. "That's what my friends call me."

"Thank you," Gabriel said, "but after all these years I don't think I could do it. Do you mind if I stay with Miz Prescott?"

"Of course not," she said. "I'm just glad you're here." Still no indication of why. "If you boys will excuse me, I think I'll head up to my room and maybe read for a while."

"Of course, Momma," I said. I rose and embraced her, for the first time in twenty years. Or was it even longer? She seemed so tiny, and yet as strong as an oak tree. Momma offered Gabriel a hug—now, there was a first—and then headed to her room.

"I'll stop in later to see if you need anything," Esther said.

"Don't worry about me, Esther," Momma said. "You get some rest." And she was gone.

Gabriel and I sat up with Esther for an hour or so after Momma went to bed. There wasn't really all that much to say, and yet it was wonderful to sit quietly with an old friend and just enjoy her presence. Esther poured Gabriel and me each a splash of Daddy's cognac, and one for herself, at my urging. "Kit, your momma is dealing with this well. You don't need to worry about her. But if you hadn't come? That would be another story."

"I'm here, Essie. Just promise you'll tell me how I'm doing," I said.

"You'll know," she said.

Gabriel and I went up to my room, stripped, and got into my old bed. We clung to each other, urgently. I don't think we said a single word, either of us. We just held each other until we fell asleep.

We were up early the next morning—about 6:00. A quick shower and we were downstairs in the kitchen. Esther got there before us, of course. The coffee was made, and there were wonderful breakfast smells swirling through the room. She had a new helper, a fresh-faced black kid. "Kit, please meet Daniel Jenkins." And we finished the introductions all around. "My preacher—you remember the Reverend Jones—told me this boy wants to become a chef. And so I said, 'Send him to me and I'll teach him everything I know. And then, when he's ready, he can move on.' "

"Daniel," I said, "You have the very best teacher. Not that I'm much of a testament to her skill. But I can assure you she will prepare you for life." Daniel seemed touched that we were making any sort of fuss over him. He was shy, and he excused himself to return to the kitchen. And I prayed that this sweet kid might have a real future with dreams granted.

Loss is hungry work. We fortified ourselves. Momma came downstairs for a sip of coffee and a few bites of buttered toast. "Your daddy will be wide awake by now," Momma said. "Let's go see him. The three of us."

"Of course, Momma," I said. I shot Gabriel a glance, but it contained only questions. No answers. The three of us headed upstairs to the sickroom. A hospital bed was installed and some electronic monitoring equipment—whatever was available in 1990. Momma and Daddy both would have insisted on the best. The night nurse was just leaving as the day nurse signed on. There was sunlight in the room, but not enough fresh air. There never does seem to be enough fresh air in sickrooms.

Daddy was propped up in bed looking alert but otherwise appropriate to the situation. Momma went over and sat on the side of the bed, took his hand, and said, "Freddy, you look much stronger this morning. I'm sure of it."

"Thank you, Vinni," he said, "but I need to talk to the boys."

"Of course, Freddy," she said. "They're right here." Momma stood up and turned to me. She indicated the sickbed, and then she walked away to the other side of the room.

I sat down where Momma had just sat, and I took Daddy's hand, just as she had done. It seemed natural. I probably hadn't touched his hand since the handshake I got when I headed off to college. But I took his hand. Instinctively. "Kit, I have to talk to you," he said.

"Of course, Daddy, I'm here."

He studied my face, and then said, "Kit, how did you manage to grow so handsome?"

"Good breeding, I guess."

"Kit, we didn't always see eye-to-eye . . ." And then he started to cough. The nurse didn't seem particularly alarmed. She just added a little morphine to his IV. It calmed him right away.

"Daddy, save your strength," I said.

"No, this has to be said. It was Esther who turned me around, wouldn't you know it. She looked me straight in the eye one day and said, 'Mr. Prescott, just because you say or do a thing, that doesn't make it right.' I've known for a lot of years I was wrong. At first I was too stubborn to tell you. And then too embarrassed. And look at me now. There's no more putting it off. I couldn't leave this unsaid: Kit, I was wrong. About you, and Gabriel, and lots of things. But I've loved you since the day you were born, and you've made me very proud. I won't ask your forgiveness. That would be too much."

"There's none needed, Daddy," I said.

"Let me talk to Gabriel," he said. I slipped away and urged Gabriel into the bedside position. But I didn't go far. This I had to hear. "Gabriel," he said, "I wish we could have been friends. It's too late for that, but I want you to know that I understand. Kit's momma told me years ago. And she always was a hell-of-a-lot smarter than I am. You've made my son very happy. And I think you're a wonderful man."

"Thank you, Mr. Prescott," Gabriel said. "Kit's happiness is one of the few things I've ever wanted."

"Kit, come back here," Daddy said. "I have to talk to you about my will." Gabriel rose from the sickbed, squeezed my shoulder, and then left the room. I slipped back to the bedside. "My lawyer's son, Richard, is running the office now. You went to school with him, didn't you?"

"Yes, Daddy."

"Talk to Richard. It's simple, really. There are a few bequests: to Esther; my secretary; and two other employees who were with me a long time. The rest goes to you, with the provision, of course, that your momma wants for nothing as long as she lives."

"Of course, Daddy, but I don't need anything. Gabriel and I have everything we need."

"That's not it, son. Please listen to me!" He sputtered a bit, but the nurse seemed to think he was okay without more drugs. He settled down, and then he said, "I think you'll be surprised to learn how much I'm leaving. There has to be a point to it. It has to do some good."

"But, Daddy, why me?" I asked.

"Because you're my son. And because you'll know what to do. I wanted to build the best house in Claysville. And I did it. If you like it, then live in it. It's yours. If you want to turn it into a home for unwed mothers, then do it! Talk to Richard, but I think there's more money than you ever imagined. Spend it! Do the right thing. Maybe I didn't always know the stuff you're made of, but I do now."

"Daddy, you need to rest. We'll talk some more tomorrow if you want." I motioned to the nurse and suggested maybe something to help him sleep.

"I love you, Daddy. Always did."

"That's what your momma told me. I guess she's smarter than I thought."

"She married you, didn't she?"

"I don't know how smart that was, but we made you, didn't we?"

"And I'm glad you did."

"So am I."

"Rest, Daddy. I'll check on you later."

Momma came back to the bedside, and I slipped out of the room. I ran down the stairs to find Gabriel. He was in the kitchen. With Esther. Where else was the heart of that house? I grabbed him and said, "Thank you, Angel, for coming with me. But now you must leave."

"Kitten, how could I abandon you at this moment?"

"Easily. I'm calling a cab. Let's get you to Greensboro/Winston-Salem. They have more flights than Raleigh/Durham, I think. Get the next one. They always have an extra seat in first class. Go! Go now!

Get home! Finish your work! Make us proud! Us, I said. Go! I'll be at the opening if I have to come dragging a casket."

"Kitten, you're a marvel," he said.

"Is this a revelation?"

"No, just an affirmation. And always worth remembering," he said. "Thank God you're always with me when I'm painting. Just behind my right ear. And I know exactly where that last canvas needs to go."

"Well then, get the fuck out of Claysville and go paint it!" I said. And he did.

Chapter Fourteen

The next two days were challenging, of course. Daddy was up and down. Mostly down. Esther was solid, of course. Momma was stoic. We had said what needed to be said, mostly, and the rest of it was just waiting. I phoned Gabriel at least twice a day. I tried not to bother him while he was painting, so I rarely called the studio. Instead I phoned him at Bank Street early in the morning or in the evening when I figured he'd be home. He sounded solid, creative, productive. Knowing that Gabe was finishing the work for the new show gave me welcome peace of mind.

My fourth day in Claysville I showed up early in the sickroom, as before. And that was the morning the fluid in Daddy's lungs got the better of him. He simply stopped breathing. There were a few false alarms. He had no intention of giving up easily. And the nurse told me the morphine not only calmed him but strengthened his heart. It seemed almost cruel. And yet? It felt like hours. But even Daddy couldn't avoid the inevitable. And his ordeal was finally over. Momma sat with him for a few minutes, kissed him, patted his hand one last time, and then went to her room.

I stood looking at what was left of my father and wondered why he always seemed so formidable. I wondered if he really loved me, as he said. And I wondered if I really loved him. I took Momma's place at the bedside, touched Daddy's hand—one last time—and removed his wedding band. I knew it needed to be put aside somewhere safe. The drama was all over, and yet his flesh was still soft and warm. I had no idea about my feelings. Not a clue.

Esther looked in on Momma and then met me in the kitchen. The two of us sat quietly. There was nothing to say. The quiet felt comforting. I looked out on the back lawn. The early rays of sunlight dancing on the surface of the pool promised a beautiful new day. The medical team swiftly arranged for the removal of the body. And they dismantled all the equipment. By noon it was as if nothing had happened in that room.

Death notices and obituaries were all written and arranged well in advance. The pastor and the funeral director both came to see Momma just after lunchtime. They hadn't planned to arrive together, but it worked out well. They suggested Saturday for the funeral. Momma agreed. And they took care of the rest. There was really nothing for me to do. I didn't even phone Gabriel immediately. I didn't want to distract him from his work. I figured the news would keep until evening. I got an afternoon phone call from the lawyer. "I'm sorry for your loss," he said.

"Thank you, Richard," I said. "I'm just glad his suffering is over." It was a simple declaration, and an honest one.

"Of course," he said. "Kit, I'd like to talk with you as soon as possible. I think your father told you a little about his will, but you need to hear the whole story. Would you like me to come by the house? I could stop by tomorrow afternoon. Or you're welcome to come to the office if you feel you could use a change of scenery."

"Thanks, Richard. That's very kind," I said. "Yes, I think I would like to get out a bit. What time should I come?"

"How about 2:00?"

"Perfect. See you then," I said. I went to find Esther, to see if I could be of any help. There would be a steady stream of mourners coming to pay calls to Momma. Esther had everything under control, of course, so I decided to go to the Y for a swim. It was a day for a real pool and real laps. I got into Daddy's car. I hadn't driven a Cadillac since I was sixteen. I hadn't driven much at all since I sold the Oldsmobile in 1972. Just the occasional rental car. Daddy's new Cadillac was smaller than I remembered from the years I lived in that house. But just as luxurious. Daddy always did like the best. Leather seats, power everything. And the air conditioning and the sound systems had evolved into living-room quality. I wouldn't be dealing with headlights or windshield wipers or other controls that had been relocated over the years. I was fine.

As I drove to the Y, I looked around at Claysville and marveled at the changes. All the open fields and cow pastures were gone. And the woods, too, most of them, except where Momma and Daddy lived. The buildings that replaced them seemed charmless. I wondered how much of this was Daddy's doing. Surely much of the open land belonged to him at some point. And the construction? I had no idea what was his and what land had been sold. Perhaps Richard would fill me in. Most of all I wondered about the deep hatred I felt for Claysville all those years. Was it justified? And what was the cost—to me and to Gabriel both—of maintaining all that negativity? Could I consider a truce?

The pool at the Y was just as I remembered it. The water worked its magic. My swim was long and meditative. And as I drove back to the house, I felt strong and peaceful. Whatever else the day had to offer, I would be ready.

The drive into town the next afternoon confirmed my impressions of how Claysville had changed. I felt a bit like a fish out of water, but I had to figure out how to swim my way to the lawyer's office anyway. The Johnsons—father and son—had taken a floor of a newish high-rise—Claysville high-rise, that is, no more than seven stories. I was ushered into smart-looking rooms by an attractive young secretary. She brought me an espressoy. And Richard came right out to invite me into his comfortable office.

We settled in. "I don't know how much you know about your father's finances," he said.

"Nothing, actually," I said, "but what he told me on his deathbed."

"I'll give you the capsule version to start. When we were schoolboys in the '50s your father still owned thousands of acres of Prescott land, all over the county. Some of it he sold off, gradually, and some of it he held onto. The parcels he kept earn some of the highest commercial rents in the state. And when he sold, he put the proceeds into the stock market. It's always up-and-down, of course, but he had excellent instincts for what to buy and when to sell. And he ended up with a securities portfolio that's valued today—we just updated it—at about $500M."

"Shit!" I said.

"And that's just the securities," Richard said. "The real estate holdings are harder to evaluate, but there's maybe even, well, conservatively, another $200M there. It's a sizable estate."

"Richard," I said. "This is crazy. I had no idea. And I have no idea how to deal with it."

"Take your time, Kit. You don't have any decisions to make right away. The securities and the real estate are all managed. Everything is solid. Your father's will goes to probate in a few days, and by next month it should all be settled. The will, that is. But then there's always red tape—notices, periods of time for claimants against the estate to respond, all of that. We're not expecting any problems. We don't know of any mistresses or illegitimate heirs—that sort of thing. It looks like a clean process. But it could take a year to finalize, anyway. Even two years.

"Also," Richard said, "we helped your father create a trust—with you as administrator. The trust has already absorbed much of the estate, including the house. I think you know he didn't want to bother your mother with inheritance matters. So we began to transfer assets, gradually, some years back. Your father's estate is now as close as possible to zero inheritance tax."

"Richard," I said. "My head is swimming." And of course swimming in an Olympic-sized pool was exactly where I wanted to be at that moment. It would have to wait.

Bruce K Beck

"There's nothing you have to do just now, Kit," Richard said. "Call me in a month, or whenever you decide to come back to town. I can lay out the entire trust plan for you. But only when you're ready. Meanwhile, we're the executors, so I can release funds for immediate expenses."

"I don't need anything," I said, "but what about my mother?"

"The household expenses will be paid regularly, as always. If she needs anything, she only has to ask. The funeral expenses are paid. Anything else that comes up will be forwarded to us. So she won't have to deal with any of it. We cut a check for $10K for you this morning. There are always expenses, so take it, and let me know if there's anything else you need."

"Richard," I said. "You've been so kind. I have to fly home to New York on Sunday, but I'll come back in two weeks, tops. And then we'll talk."

"Safe journey," he said. I took the check, of course. I'm not stupid. And then I headed back to the house for the vigil. At least Daddy wasn't laid out in the parlor. Funeral homes are a great invention, I always thought. It gets the body out of the house so that people don't have to trip over it right up until the interment. Momma and I went to Rand & Thomas's on two evenings for viewings and sympathy. We both dressed for it and got through it, because it's what people do. I hate funerals. Daddy hated funerals. He didn't even like wakes, though he had nothing against drinking. But he had to show up at the church in his best black suit, and so did I. And we both played our roles.

After the burial there was a reception at the church. I wasn't much interested in the expressions of sympathy from the parishioners, but these were Momma's people. Things needed to be said. It's how it's done. I accepted it, for her sake. And then we came home. Momma took a little nap. I changed out of my black suit and took a mini swim in the pool. And then Esther made a little supper for Momma and me.

"How are you feeling, Momma?" I asked.

"A little tired," she said.

"No, I mean how are you *feeling*?" I said.

"Well, darling, you may not understand this . . . what am I saying? You understand just about everything. You always did. When you were about six, I had to start having adult conversations with you. Nothing childish would do. Kit, I loved that man so much! I made him my whole life. And then when you arrived, everything seemed perfect. And I wanted it to be forever. Well, our forever turned out to be forty-two years. Some people get more, and some less. And now? I don't know. I have to start a new life."

"I'd like to help," I said.

"Kit, just having you here this week has been a godsend."

"Momma, I have to fly home tomorrow. Gabriel's show opens in a few days. I have to be there," I said.

"Of course you do," she said. "Will you send me some photos? I'd love to see his work."

"I'll do better than that," I said. "I'll buy you one. I know the artist. I can get a deal."

"Kit, if only we had . . ."

"Momma, we don't have time for 'if only' any more. That's no way to live. I have to go tomorrow, but I'll fly back in about a week. Or a week-and-a-half. Momma, how much do you know about Daddy's finances?"

"I don't want you to think your Daddy treated me as if I'm stupid. We had a much more equal partnership than you probably know. But he didn't want to worry me with business matters. So he told me as little as possible, whether it was up or down. I knew, of course, when he made a killing in the stock market. It was obvious. And I knew when he had losses. That was obvious, too. But I never looked at the books. That's not how we did things."

"Well, Momma, Richard showed *me* the books this week, and there's a fortune there. We have a lot of decisions to make."

"I do know your Daddy wanted *you* to make those decisions. He told me that. I will not interfere."

"Momma, this is your life and your legacy—your joint legacies. It has to be what you want. All of it," I said.

"Kit, darling, I can't begin to tell you how thrilled I was when your daddy told me the terms of his new will. And I said to him, 'Freddy, you've done the perfect thing. That boy will do you proud.'"

"You knew?" I asked.

"Of course," she said. "Well, you're right. Let's not talk about the past. You fly home tomorrow and take care of what's precious to you. And then come back to us when you can, and we'll talk about the future."

I started to weep. Momma had shed all her tears in recent weeks, but I had held onto mine. Until she gave me permission to shed them. Momma got up quietly and came around behind my chair, putting her arms around me and resting her head on mine. I couldn't remember when—if ever—I had felt that maternal embrace. It felt natural. It felt real.

Chapter Fifteen

Gabriel's show was so beautiful I grinned from ear to ear all evening long at the opening. The last canvas he finished—the one I sent him home to paint—was the one that created the most buzz. Gabriel didn't show it to me when I got home from Claysville. He asked me to wait until the opening, when it would be displayed properly, with the others in the collection. I agreed, of course.

We were the first ones in the door that evening as the gallerist was approving the final lighting choices and making sure the caterer had the bar under control. Gabriel took me through the first rooms rather quickly. I had seen all the pictures as he was painting them, mostly. They looked wonderful. I wouldn't have changed a thing in the sequence or the presentation. And then he led me to the last room and the last picture. It was a delicious, painterly, long, lean male nude. It was really more about color than it was about representing the human body, yet it was perhaps the most erotic painting I've ever seen.

"I painted it from memory," Gabriel said.

"Yes, but from what memory?" I said.

"You don't recognize yourself?" he asked.

Well, sure enough, it *was* me. Or at least the me I always wanted to be. The me I always wanted to be for Gabriel. It was—heroic, actually. It was splendid. I can't compare Gabriel's work to J. S. Sargent—they're a century apart and just as removed in their visions. But there was something about my portrait that reminded me of Sargent: the detail Gabriel lavished on the face and the hands while the rest of the body was merely suggested by extravagant swirls of paint. And the background was so dark there could be no distractions; no questions about where the eye should focus.

The picture was priced high—$50K. That was high in those days for Gabriel's work. It would be nothing now. Gabriel hoped to keep the picture as much as he hoped to sell it. But sell, it did. In the first hour. The buyer wished to remain anonymous. That was not surprising; many collectors value their privacy. We were both thrilled by the sale and saddened to see the picture go.

Gabriel was radiant. Success certainly agreed with him. The entire evening was a swirl of pride and well-wishers. I knew it was a milestone for Gabriel. A career high. A new level of acceptance and respect. The timing seemed perfect to me. He had worked so long and hard, and with such focus and dedication. And he would now see a return on that investment. The gallerist was beaming, too. He didn't have to tell us that the opening was a great success, and that sales were even better than hoped.

We laughed—a lot—as we made our way home after too much champagne and celebration. We were still laughing as we stripped off our clothes and fell into bed. Poor Buster missed his walk that night. A garden visit would have to do. It was a Friday night, so we could sleep late in the morning. More good timing. And then I'd give Buster an extra-long walk, I promised myself.

As soon as we had enjoyed a little celebratory breakfast—I laid in a supply of smoked salmon and cream cheese and capers and all of that, in preparation—Gabriel and I both threw on some clothes and brought out Buster's leash. He was delighted. And our little family had a joyous outing. Life was good. It was almost enough to erase fears of the future— the unknown waiting in Claysville.

The next week, just before I headed back to North Carolina, Karl asked me to stop by. I accepted with pleasure, of course. He let me into his apartment and I embraced him warmly, as always. "Karl, thank you so much for minding Buster. I know he can be a handful, but he adores you."

"It's mutual. And speaking of adoration . . ." Karl turned me around to face the wall opposite the windows. And there—floor to ceiling—stood the portrait. My portrait!

"Karl, this is crazy!" I said.

"Kit, I hope you'll forgive me. I had to have it. I won't keep it long. Maybe a few years. And then I'll give it to you. And you'll know what to do with it. But I had to possess it."

"You could have the original at any moment, Karl. You know that," I said.

"It's kind of you to say that, Kit, but . . . well . . . that's not the nature of our friendship. I suppose we have to tell Gabriel it's here."

"He'll be honored."

"It's just that this picture is the best of both of you. And I've loved you two for nearly twenty years.

I had no choice. My checkbook flew right out of my pocket."

"Karl, you're a madman," I said.

"A madman *and* your Fairy Godfather, don't forget." As if I could.

I hated leaving Gabriel so soon after his gallery opening. He offered to join me on my return to Claysville, but I made him promise to stay in New York to take care of business. There are always events that follow a successful opening—requests for interviews, additional sales, commission offers. I didn't want him to miss a thing. I assured him there would be plenty of time to deal with Claysville in the months to come.

I told Gabriel about Daddy's will, of course. And he said to me, "Kitten, it's what you were born for."

"Please, Angel," I said. "After all these years, please don't talk to me about white-boy privilege."

"That couldn't be farther from what I'm trying to tell you: Kit, you're the only man in or out of Claysville who can figure out what that town needs. And, obviously, your daddy knew that, too. Don't fight it. I wish I could help you with it. I *will* help you with it. I'll do anything you ask—if you'll just accept it."

And, perhaps, I did accept it, maybe just at that moment. And my return trip was lighter than I had imagined. It was an evening flight that got in late. Esther had asked the gardener to let me in. And I trod those familiar steps up to my old room with yet another layer of life under my belt. And it was all I could do to get my clothes off before I slipped into bed and conked out.

Chapter Sixteen

At breakfast I greeted Esther, of course. And
Daniel. He offered to make a special omelet for me
with fresh herbs from the garden. They had planted
tarragon that year, and chives, and chervil, and he
was keen to use them. I accepted with pleasure. The
omelet was perfect. Not to mention Esther's biscuits.
It would have been impossible to nurse old grudges
in such surroundings, even for someone so inclined.

"What does this town need?" I asked Esther, after
I enjoyed a delicious meal. She sat with me for a few
minutes. Momma had started taking breakfast in
her room. The house was quiet.

"Where should I start?" Esther asked.

"At the beginning, please," I said.

"Kit, remember how much you loved your art
classes? They don't really have them anymore. Not
even in the white schools—sorry, the *integrated*
schools. The black schools were always touch-and-
go.   Gabriel got support from some courageous
teachers. Those old ladies are history. It's over. Mu-
sic? Forget it. Drama? Not anymore. You see
Daniel out there?" Esther asked, *sotto voce.* "That
boy would be in a drug den somewhere if he weren't
here."

Shit! I thought. But what I said was, "Esther,
leave it to you to tell me the truth."

"I think that's the nature of our relationship," she said. I looked at her with such a sense of hopelessness that she took my chin in her hand, just like the old days, and said, gently, "Well, little man, what are you going to do about it?"

Did I start to cry? Right there at the breakfast table? Maybe a little. But I also realized, truly, that decisions needed to be made, and that I would make them. But not at that moment. I went up to see Momma and took her a yellow rose from the garden. She invited me to sit next to her. Esther had brought up an extra coffee cup, just in case. Momma poured me some coffee and added just the right amount of warm milk. Even though we had spent so little time together in the last years, she remembered how I like my breakfast coffee.

"How are you feeling, Momma?" I asked.

"Strong," she said. "Sad, but strong. And how are you, darling?" she asked.

"Momma, I wish I had an answer for that question. I don't, but I can tell you Gabriel's opening was triumphant," I said."

"I knew it would be," she said. "I'm so proud, for both of you."

"I know I promised to bring you your very own Gabriel Williamson painting, but, well, everything seems so up-in-the-air. I'll figure it out, very soon," I said.

"Choose something that will fit into my new apartment," she said.

"But, Momma," I said. "This is your home."

"Used to be," she said, "but now with your daddy gone, it's just a big old house. I'm thinking next month. Kit, I'm not sure you ever really understood our family."

"Momma, I don't think I've understood much of anything about family. Certainly not when I was a child. Our family? Other than Bullards and Prescotts, I had no idea what was going on. But when I met Gabriel and asked him to be my family, and he agreed, then that felt right. And then we did it. God damn it, we did it! And I will not apologize for it."

"Nor should you," she said. "I just wish we could have been better friends, through the years. No, I think that's not what it's about. I wish *you and your daddy* could have had the bond he wanted. He would have done anything for you."

"I would have done anything for *him*! Why do you think I learned to swim? Only because it pleased him. And when he reached for me at the edge of the pool when I finished a lap, I felt like a prince. I don't know. I'm sure I worshiped him when I was a little kid. I remember looking at you two when you were headed to a dance at the Club. Daddy was so handsome and you were so beautiful, like a princess. I thought you were magical."

"Your Daddy was the handsomest man I ever clapped eyes on, until you grew up, of course. He knew that you became better looking than he was. He pretended to be gruff about it, but mostly he was bursting with pride because he was the source. Because we made you."

"I don't know exactly when my feelings started to change," I said. "Momma, look at me. I'm hardly a communist. But I couldn't understand what Daddy was doing with his real estate deals, and whatever else was going on. I didn't *want* to know. And now?"

"Kit, darling, I have to tell you the saddest part of this: What you never understood is that you and your daddy were cut from the same cloth. You two were more alike than you ever knew. Than *he* ever knew. But the difference is that *he* figured it out—maybe only a few years ago. And you?"

"Momma, I thought Esther was the only one in this house who could floor me with the truth. But I was wrong. Yet again," I said.

"When you were a teenager and you and your daddy started to lock horns, I dismissed it. That's what fathers and sons do, after all. I just never thought we wouldn't survive it," Momma said. She had a faraway look in her eyes. The sadness of it gripped my heart.

"Well, I'm here, and you're here," I said. "What can I do to make up for the mistakes of the past?"

"Don't be dramatic, darling," she said. "Just do what needs to be done. You'll figure it out. I asked Esther if she'd move with me—to an apartment. I'm used to her taking care of my needs, of course, but this time we'll be more like roommates. We'll find someone to help with the housework and whatever else we need—both of us. I'm looking forward to it. And I'm looking forward to seeing what you'll do with this house. I have just as much faith in your judgment as your daddy did."

"I'll try to justify your confidence, Momma. I need to get back to New York soon. Is there anything you need from me just now?"

"The lawyer's boy, Richard, calls me every few days. He and Esther and I will get the move all sorted out. When will we see you again?" she asked.

"I was just trying to figure that out. I do have a job, and I've been AWOL a lot this month. I have to get home and make some decisions. I can probably fly back in about two weeks," I said.

"Lovely," she said. "Go safely and come back to us when you can."

The trip home was easy enough, but my brain was in high gear the whole time. I usually nap on flights. Not that one. When I got home to Bank Street, Gabriel's welcome was precious, indeed. And Buster was also delighted to see me. I was so overwhelmed by the decisions facing me that I didn't say much that evening. Which is not like me, of course. Gabriel let me be quiet. We had a good meal at the same little French restaurant that hosted our first celebratory dinner in New York, nearly twenty years earliers. Yes, it was still there. Village institutions like that are sometimes long-lived.

"Angel, I'm feeling a bit overwhelmed," I said when we had finished dinner and were picking at des,sert.

"Of course you are, Kitten. Just take a deep breath. And let's head home. You've been away, and I'm dying to make love to you. First things first."

We paid the check and got out of the restaurant as quickly as possible. We sprinted home, let ourselves in, and whipped off our clothes like teenagers. I had to let Buster out into the garden, as much as I'd have preferred to ignore him until later. But as soon as Buster finished his garden business I got him in, locked the garden door, and dove into our bed. Gabriel's body against mine was both familiar and like the first time. His kiss was just as it had always been: home.

I only topped Gabriel a few times, in the last decade. He accepted it, but I was never certain how much he really wanted it. That night, Gabriel said, "Please, Kitten, get inside."

"Angel, are you sure it's what you want?" I asked.

"Shut up and fuck me," Gabriel whispered. And I did. I gripped him, and entered him, and kissed him, and wrapped my arms around him, and rocked our bodies like a cradle. I also wept a little. And when I came, Gabriel smiled up at me and started to laugh, softly. "That's my man," he said. "He can do anything."

"You're fucking with me!" I said.

"I thought *you* were fucking with *me*," Gabriel said.

"It's the same thing, yes?"

"Yes," he said.

At breakfast the next morning I asked Gabriel to spend an hour with me, making plans. He agreed. "I don't know what to do about Claysville," I said.

"But you will," Gabriel said.

"So everyone tells me. But meanwhile, I have this job. What do I do about the Met?"

"I think you should talk to Jacques," Gabriel said. "I think you should tell him you're setting up a new nonprofit—that is what you intend to do, isn't it?"

"Shit!" I said. "Is that what I have to do?"

"Well, I'd say if it looks like a duck and quacks like a . . ."

"Spare me," I said. "But we still have to live. Daddy's estate won't be settled for a year or even more."

"In case my kitten hasn't noticed, his angel brought some funds into the family coffers lately. We're good for a while. A year? Maybe two? Kit, you're free to get on with it. If I were you, I'd make an appointment with Jacques as soon as possible. But I'm not you, as much as I'd like to be. I'm just our most ardent admirer."

"But you *are* me," I said. "You were always the best part of me."

"Thanks for that, but you're quite wrong," Gabriel said. "You've been the best part of *me* all these years, as if I didn't know. Now, go for it: Tell that prissy son of a bitch that you're leaving, and you're taking your expertise to a new venue of your creation, and that you hope to maintain a cordial relationship forever after. As if I have to coach you on bullshit."

"You're right, of course," I said. "But how am I going balance all of this?"

"Our whole life together has been a balancing act. So what's changed?" Gabriel asked. And of course he was right. Our new life would be neither more nor less mysterious than the old one. The only real difference was that my decisions would start to affect the lives of many rather than the lives of a few.

Chapter Seventeen

I did make an appointment to see Jacques de Belmonte, the director of the Met. That gave me three days to plan my strategy. Gabriel was a great sounding board for trying out my riffs. And by the scheduled meeting date I was ready. He kept me waiting only a few minutes before his secretary ushered me into his office. De Belmonte rose from his chair and greeted me warmly. Crafty old fundraisers are good at that.

"Thank you for seeing me," I said.

"Not at all, Kit," he said. "Please sit."

I got right to the point. "My father left me a large estate and a large house in North Carolina, where I grew up."

"It's a beautiful state. I've had some lovely holidays in Asheville. What will you do with it?"

"Yes, exactly. I'm creating the Frederick D. and Lavinia B. Prescott Center for the Arts in my parents' house. Claysville needs that more than anything else I could do, I think. School children, in particular, need a place to go. A place to learn. It won't be easy, of course. And it means I'll have to leave the Met. It's been my second home for nearly twenty years, and I'll miss it terribly," I said.

"Yes, I think you've been here even longer than I have. But your new venture sounds exciting, indeed. Is there anything we can do to help?" he asked.

"As a matter of fact," I said, "I hope you'll sit on the board. We'll need expert guidance, of course."

"It will be my honor," he said. "When will you leave?"

"In a few days, I think," I said. "I hate to miss working on the Edwardians show coming up in the spring, but this new project feels like the most important work of my career."

"And no doubt it will be. Congratulations, Kit. Do keep us informed of your progress. And if there's anything we can do to help, you need only ask."

"Thank you, sir," I said.

"Jacques," he said.

"Yes, thank you. You've always been very gracious to me," I said.

"And you've been a valued member of our team. I'm sure that your experience here will hold you in good stead in the future," he said.

"Yes, no doubt," I said. "Thanks again." I didn't wait for him to rise from his chair to indicate that the audience had ended. Instead I got right to my feet. A quick handshake and I was out of that office. I was quivering with excitement as I headed back to my desk to gather my thoughts and my things. I had stated my case, clearly, and gotten everything I wanted to get. It was a triumph. A mini triumph, but a triumph nonetheless. The first of many, I hoped. I couldn't wait to tell Gabriel all about it. I left work early, had a good swim, and then headed to Gabriel's studio to share the news.

In the days that followed, I refined my plans. The Prescott Center for the Arts, indeed. It had to have a mission, and a vision, not to mention renovations. There had to be programs for kids as well as programs for adults and seniors. There had to be a way to turn the main gallery space—the big rooms on the ground floor—into a party space that would become the most coveted in town. I imagined the weddings and charity balls we would host. And why not, really? The Country Club is very nice, but how could it match the scenery at the Center? It was scary, but it was also the most thrilling work of my career. Perhaps Gabriel was right. Perhaps it was the work I was born for. Here's how I set it up:

I created the office of President for myself. And Chairman of the Board of Directors. The board included Momma and Esther, and Jacques de Belmonte came through, as promised. I included the mayor of Claysville, as an ex officio board member, and the Director of City Schools, as well. I even appointed old Mr. Clay's son Matthew to the board. It seemed a good way to smooth old wounds and bring the county and the city together.

I knew there had to be a summer painting program for public school kids. I appointed Gabriel its director, of course. He accepted with grace (as always). For other programs, I would need help. And there needed to be a permanent collection. I wanted us to become an important regional museum along with our education and community outreach functions. I mined the family first—our family:

Bruce K Beck

Gabriel's little sister, Melinda, had completed Harvard and the Wharton School of Business at U. Penn. I wanted to have her as our Financial Officer and Director of Development. I had to lure her away from a good job at a nonprofit in St. Louis. But I did it. It took some doing to get Melinda to consider returning to Claysville (sound familiar?). But there was something so glorious and new about the Center that it nearly sold itself. I asked Rick—Jerry's partner—to be our accountant, to work with Melinda. He declined, citing the long-distance factor. Today it's possible to work from anywhere, but in those days proximity was still important. So we had to hire a local firm. No problem.

As for the permanent collection and its relationship to the community, I twisted another family arm: Gabriel's little brother, Aaron, studied art history at Howard and had a good job at the National Gallery, in DC. I convinced him to become the Artistic Director for the Center. I knew he would bring wisdom about gallery planning and new exhibits as well as a particular sensitivity to the needs of young black students in Claysville. And if we got that wrong, we'd be doomed to the halls of irrelevancy.

Another way we scouted talent—and one I insisted on—was sending a representative to the annual job fair at UNC that winter. I knew we could fill some junior positions there. And we did. The team was excited—and exciting. I had never been part of any team other than a swim team. But perhaps that experience helped me see the importance of each member performing at peak energy and skill. And we had that. I hadn't never occurred to me, really, that Gabriel and me as a team.

Once I could access the funds in the foundation, one of my first purchases was a small Sargent. A male nude. A collector in London had owned it for decades and was ready to sell. I knew the collector, actually. It was my job to know where every authenticated Sargent was. He contacted me first, rather than the Met. I said yes. Instantly. I'd have paid nearly anything for it, but he only asked a fair price. Done. Packed and shipped.

I had him send it to Bank Street. I told myself it was for the permanent collection. But I wanted to savor it—I wanted for Gabriel and me to savor it—as long as possible. Karl came downstairs the day the picture arrived, to help me uncrate it. I knew the picture already. I had seen it in photos and in person. Karl only knew *about* it. And as we carefully pried open the sturdy casing and brought the canvas into the light, we both gasped—Karl, because it was so beautiful, and I, because it was mine. Oddly, the only things I'd ever truly wanted were Gabriel and a Sargent. And at that moment I had both.

I had to figure a way to thank Karl for his kindness and generosity through the years. I thought about buying him a gold Rolex. But that seemed stupid and obvious. Everything I thought of seemed stupid and obvious. Eventually I simply asked him to keep the portrait, my portrait. He said he would be honored to enjoy it for the rest of his life. And he also promised to gift it to the Center in his will. Once again Karl was giving and we were taking. It seemed the nature of our relationship. And then I had another thought.

One night that fall when Karl was in town, the three of us had dinner at a favorite neighborhood spot. I asked Karl to come back to the apartment. He accepted. I had finally learned to make good coffee, if nothing else of interest in the kitchen. Buster was delighted to see Karl, of course, and they had a nice reunion. We settled in for a visit, and Buster curled up under Karl's chair and took a nap. It had been such an easy friendship, all those years. And there we were, sitting at Karl's table and looking out at his garden and feeling quite contented. I poured a little cognac as well.

"Karl," I said, "we'll never be able to thank you properly for all you've done for us, but I just created the Karl Nesbitt Fellowship. You can add Johnny's name to it if you wish. Just let me know. The interest on the endowment will put a young student through art school, all expenses paid. If you'd rather see it provide classes at the Center for several students at a time, then we can use it that way. Your choice."

"Kit, that's a lovely thing you've done. I feel honored. And, yes, do add John Simpson to the name of the fellowship. As for the purpose, I want you to decide that. Whatever you two think is the best use of the funds, then do it. I'll be content with your decision."

"Thanks, Karl. We'll do our best," I said. And I felt I had finally managed to repay—in part—a great debt.

Chapter Eighteen

I was flying by the seat of my pants, but I also reminded myself—often—that I was coaching a fabulous team of competent professionals. It took time, of course. Two years. But we walked through everything that needed to be done. Gabriel and I spent a lot of time in New York, but as often as possible we grabbed Buster and headed for Teterboro. We didn't even need to pack, really, because we had everything we needed in Claysville, too. There was a good pilot with a Lear Jet who could always seem to accommodate us, even on short notice. I thought about buying a plane. I even thought about learning to fly. But I came to my senses and gave up that idea.

Buster loved chasing the squirrels on the back lawn in Claysville. He liked Village squirrels, too, of course. But the Southern ones were even faster. He never caught one, luckily. But it wasn't for want of trying. Buster also loved the visits to Momma and Esther at their apartment. We kept Daddy's last Cadillac for ages, and Buster loved to leap into the back seat and then stick his head out the window for the short drive. I didn't know whether Momma would take to him and his high spirits, but she did seem to enjoy his visits. And, oddly enough, Buster adopted a quieter demeanor when we went visiting. He was never subdued. But he became—dare I say it?—

nearly dignified when we visited the ladies. And Buster never did a leg-lift on even one of Momma's French chairs—to my great relief.

There was so much going on at the house that Gabriel and I enjoyed those visits to Momma and Esther as much as Buster did. We had tea with them and savored the quiet. And once Buster had been through the greeting ritual—with too many hand kisses—he would settle down by Esther's chair and then never leave her side until it was time for us to say good-bye—with more hand kisses, of course— and pile back into Daddy's car for the return.

Gabriel and I tried to help with whatever needed doing at the moment. It had been so long since we actually lived in Claysville that I had no idea what to expect from local businesses. Were we perhaps too progressive, too gay, and too interracial for their tastes? Maybe even too New York? One construction company turned me down—politely—citing prior commitments. I heard the dog whistle loud and clear with no help needed from Buster. The next firm I contacted was eager for the work. And that's what counts in the long run.

Plans were drawn up, and we were off and running. The house lent itself beautifully to its new uses. The big rooms on the ground floor we converted to galleries and classrooms. Daddy's study made a perfect media room. Some of the bedrooms upstairs were just right for studios and galleries. And the smaller rooms on the third floor were easily converted to offices. It was a long, loud, and dusty process. I had lots of doubts about our choices, but it did start to come together.

There had always been pictures in the house— some that Daddy bought on their honeymoon in

Europe, and others he had acquired later. They were competent, for the most part, but nothing we really needed for the collection, other than a small Corot. And a very sweet English animal scene that might possibly be a Landseer. I asked Momma to take her favorites to her new apartment, and the rest we sold. I think she was happy for the continuity. And I did send a Gabriel Williamson for their new apartment. It was something Gabe painted just for Momma and Esther. I always have trouble doing justice to Gabriel's paintings. This one is smallish, and so full of sunlight that it always makes me grin when I see it. Like *Breakfast in the Loggia*? Perhaps.

There was just one, rather monumental piece that really needed to stay, and that was the portrait of Momma that Daddy commissioned shortly after I was born. No one in Claysville could deliver what he wanted, so he chose the best society portraitist in Winston-Salem. It's good. Very good. Not Sargent, of course, but what else is? The portrait had always hung in a place of honor in the big living room. I had it moved to the vestibule, and now it's the first work that every visitor sees. And I made it clear that it will always hang there, as long as the building stands. That portrait honors Momma and the building itself honors Daddy, I think. That's what I wanted to guarantee.

📖

I kept my old room. I wanted a place for Gabriel and me to sleep when we were in town. And what better place than the room where we made love so sweetly so many years before? Yes, I kept that room and we still sleep there. The room is big enough that I was able to add a desk and make it my office, too. I commissioned a screen from a local artist, to separate the living and working spaces. The artist is a strange and reclusive guy who lives way outside of town. He looks a bit like a rural good old boy, but his talent is another matter. We had seen some of his work, and I knew he would deliver exactly what was needed.

Jimmy Jarvis didn't see many people, but I stopped by his house/studio and tried to convince him to come by to see the space I needed to define. He agreed. Or at least I hoped he agreed. The next day one of the interns drove to Jimmy's house and coaxed him into his car. Jimmy looked quite spooked when I went out front to greet him. But he came upstairs anyway. I showed him where I wanted the screen, and he said, "How about I depict the Battle of Prescott County?" I wasn't certain whether he was referring to the Revolution or the Civil War or maybe some skirmish of his own imagining. But it sounded perfect, so I said, "Yes, please. Whatever you want to paint." And he agreed.

I didn't know what to expect. I hadn't even been able to ask him how long it would take. But I got a carpenter to build the actual screen and deliver it to Jimmy. I could have had something finely crafted from walnut or fruitwood in High Point. But instead, I went to the guy who made pine boxes for bargain funerals in Claysville, and I asked him to build me a room divider in six panels. It was exactly what the space needed, and the carpenter built it and carted it over to Jimmy's.

I paid Jimmy in advance for the commission. I thought it only fair. There were people at the house who advised me against the prepayment, suggesting that Jimmy might go on an alcoholic bender and neglect the work. I had no intention of starting our Arts Center by doubting artists. I paid. I waited. And one day, about three months later, Jimmy's sister phone to tell us it was ready. He didn't have a phone, but his sister, who looked in on him every few days, did. As soon as she called, I tried to figure out how to get the screen to the house.

The screen was much too big for Daddy's car, so I went to the two brothers with a van who were doing landscaping work on the grounds. I even remember their names, for some reason (perhaps because they were both so very cute). I gave John and Jeff Richards a sort of crash course in fine-art moving, plus a lot of blankets and other padding. And I asked them to treat the screen as if it were as precious as their mother's best china. I think they understood. The screen arrived at the house perfectly intact.

So, the Battle of Prescott County—is it about the Revolution? Yes. Is it about the Civil War? Yes. And is it about other people and situations? Yes. Most assuredly. It's about Native Americans and African slaves and Planters and Poor White Trash and every other *flora* or *fauna* you can imagine that ever occupied this landscape, including the famous Siamese twins. If he had been Michelangelo on his back in the Sistine Chapel, Jimmy couldn't have touched more bases. It's wonderful work. And it's only just one of many extraordinary pieces that we acquired, or that we enabled. Every student who comes to the Center gets to see it. It would seem an odd workday if I didn't get at least a few taps on my door from guides who want to show it to their groups.

Bruce K Beck

Every day that I'm in Claysville I get to sit at that desk and feel all that delicious rambunctiousness going on behind me. I won't give it up, but I also feel—keenly—that it is not mine. It belongs to the Center. And if a school group is scheduled to arrive on a morning when I had hoped to sleep late, then poor me! The students come first.

While the construction was underway, Gabriel, Aaron, and I set out to build the permanent collection. There had to be a regional focus, but we wanted the flexibility to include anything beautiful we could acquire. The Met sold us six canvases from their storage collection, pieces I knew about but hadn't imagined could be ours. These were paintings—portraits and battle scenes, mainly—that were painted in the South or had belonged to rich Southerners. The Met, with all its vast holdings, had no use for these works. And yet they were perfect for us. Jacques de Belmonte came through. Deals were done. We also bought some gorgeous American furniture and some sculptures. Again, these were pieces that begged to come out of hiding in New York and see the light of day in Claysville.

There were other outsiders in our area—not so very different from Jimmy Jarvis—whose work we researched. Aaron wanted to do an outsider gallery. I thought that was perfect. We bought some pieces and commissioned some others. This was a segment of American Art I had been ignorant of until we started our search. I began to hear stories and to meet artists who were, well, different. Some were black and some were white, with a healthy admixture of Native American. Many were reclusive. Some had been classified as retarded. Some were bat-shit crazy. But they all had extraordinary talent. And that was their admission to our gallery.

I knew we had to have a Gabriel Williamson Gallery. He is, after all, our most important regional artist. Gabe was pleased. I talked to Aaron about it, of course, and everyone else on the team. I had one requirement: I was determined that visitors have an experience like the ones at the Met or the National Gallery: I'm talking about walking to the next doorway and turning to see, suddenly, in the next gallery, or even two galleries away, BAM! Whistler's *White Girl*, or van Dyke's *Marchesa Grimaldi*, or, of course, Sargent's *Madame X*.

We would, in the future, have the perfect canvas for that kind of discovery, that kind of drama. We would have my portrait. And meanwhile we had our choice of several of Gabriel's best works, any one of which would do the job admirably. I never twisted an arm. Everyone agreed. Aaron found a local architect to design a new space to adjoin the house. It's all about openness and light. It's stark, actually. There are no distractions. Gabriel's pictures look wonderful in that space. And every visitor gets the little tingle in the spine at stepping into a doorway and turning to discover something surprising and wonderful.

Once the construction was completed—most of it—we hung what we had acquired of the new collection and tried to make it look at least a little like a museum. And it did. And it was time to show it off. There would be new additions and countless changes to come, but it was time to celebrate. Momma came to the dedication, looking radiant. She had seen some of the changes to the building, over the last two years, but the transformation of a mansion into a cultural institution is dramatic, indeed. She seemed devoid of any sentimentality about the past, and genuinely pleased with what we had done.

I invited Momma to say a few words before we cut the ribbon, just around the corner from her portrait. She agreed, and we popped the corks. "Our son, Christopher, has made me proud every day of his life, but never more so than today. I only wish his father could be here to see it. My husband's fondest wish, in his last years, was that Christopher would do something grand for the people of Claysville. Claysville was his home his entire life, and he loved it. He also loved this house, but not as much as the idea of its doing some good for this town. And now it will. My husband would be thrilled and honored that this new Arts Center bears his name. As I am, too." Momma raised her glass and said, "To Christopher!" And everyone followed suit.

It was a weepy occasion, of course. So much work. So much history. So much work to follow! Jacques was there. And the rest of the team, of course. And everyone with any power or influence in Claysville I could think of to invite. And a group of school kids to take the first tour. Esther congratulated me; she was beaming with pride. It was almost enough to cover the fact that she didn't really look all that well. As soon as I could get away, I led her to the old kitchen to show her the blueprints for the new one: The Esther M. Graves School of Culinary Arts. We had broken ground just a few months before, on the back lawn. In another six months or so, there would be a state-of-the-art facility that could help all the Daniels in that town to realize their dreams.

"Essie, none of this could have happened without you," I said.

"I'm glad you think so," she said, "but I only did what people do for people they love."

We sipped our champagne and enjoyed the moment, and then I said, "Essie, forgive me for saying this, but you don't look well. What's going on?"

"Old age," she said. "Just wait."

"What does the doctor say?" I asked. "Who are you seeing, one of the Kronauers?"

"As a matter of fact, they do take colored patients these days. But no, I'm seeing a very nice young woman who's the daughter of an old friend from church. And she says my systems are shutting down and there's not much to do about it."

"Shit!" I said. "You're coming to New York next week. I won't accept that. We'll find you the best doctor in town. You deserve decades more of robust good health. I will not stand by and watch you slip away from us. I won't do it!"

Esther took my chin in her hand, just like in the old days, and said, "Well, little man, there are some things even you can't fix. Though this might be the first one." I felt devastated. I turned into a mess, which was doing no one any good.

"You're coming to New York," I said quietly.

"No."

"Yes,"

"Give it up, Kit," she said. "You'll not win this battle."

"If you won't do it for yourself, then do it for Momma," I said.

"The Good Lord gave your momma all the strength she needs. And when I'm gone, she'll get on with her life just fine. You'll see."

"Then will you do it for me?" I asked.

"Not even for you, the child I raised but never bore—the most precious love of my life. I've seen enough, Kit. I've seen you grow into a fine, handsome man. I've seen you take on responsibilities. I've seen you do the right thing. It's enough. I'm ready."

Chapter Nineteen

We were in Claysville when Esther died. Even though it was not a surprise, Esther's death was still shocking to both of us. She meant so much to Gabriel and me through the years. Buster had fallen in love with her, too. Even he seemed uncharacteristically subdued when we got the news. We headed to the apartment. Just as Esther promised, Momma took it in her stride. I wondered if I'd ever learn that kind of acceptance. That's it, I think. Acceptance. Resignation is an animal of a different stripe. It bears at least a small portion of resentment. No. That's not the way to do it, I'm sure.

Esther was so peaceful about the end that I had to will myself to find some of that peace. And I did, I think. But I also did some wrangling: I convinced her pastor—the Reverend Jones, *Jr.*—that she must be buried next to her school instead of in his churchyard. I prevailed. A generous donation to the church in her memory helped. And it also took money to get a special city waiver allowing human remains on undesignated property. But, of course, it was the right thing to do—which often helps. Esther's little man came through with flying colors.

The next few years—in New York City, anyway—seemed odd in that while tolerance was on the rise, so was hate. Greenwich Village had always felt like a haven, an oasis of acceptance. Gabriel and I both had felt wonderfully safe there, since our arrival in 1972. And yet, by the mid-'90s we had to rethink our lives and our routines. Gay men—and even men suspected of being gay—were victims of bashings at an alarming rate. There was a racial component as well. There often is, where hate is concerned. We never imagined we had been living in some lotus land, but we still found the changes surprising. The hate speech from the previous decade—from the AIDS wars—fanned some flames, no doubt.

We stopped our late-night dog walks entirely. It no longer seemed safe. And we stopped going out after dark unless we could hop into a cab and go right to the restaurant or the theatre and then cab it home afterward. We didn't know whether it was safer for us to be alone on the street, or if the safety-in-numbers rule applied. We wondered if the two of us, walking together—an interracial gay couple—might provoke an incident. We had never taken our differences all that seriously until New York, of all places, forced us to—after twenty-five years together. It was disturbing. But like all situations, it became the new normal.

We were in Claysville on 9/11. I was glad to be away from it. We phoned Javier, not because he could do anything about the gray toxic dust that settled over lower Manhattan, but because we hoped he'd head uptown to spend the next few months with his family in the Bronx. Time and a few good soaking rains eventually washed away the worst of it. On Bank Street, that is. The next time we were home and Buster bounded into the garden to explore all the wonders of nature he had been missing, we hoped it was safe. We hoped it was safe for Gabriel and me, too. As much as I look for assurances, there were none to be had.

Karl was with his sister in Connecticut when he died—quietly, in his sleep, she said. Gabriel and I were at Bank Street much of that winter, so we only had a short journey to the funeral. It was a cruel season for us, actually. Buster developed a nasty cancer that began to sap his strength. He was obviously in pain, so we had to put him down. It wasn't easy, saying good-bye to him. And it wasn't easy— with the soil half frozen—digging a grave for Buster in the garden. But we managed it, and then we headed up to Connecticut for the next good-bye.

Somehow we had never met Karl's sister, Emma, in all those years. And yet we were like old friends as we mourned Karl's loss. She was exactly the woman I expected—from Karl's descriptions of her. There was a definite family resemblance, and she seemed to share his quiet, kindly façade with a wicked sense of play just beneath the surface. After the funeral we returned to her house, and she handed me a letter. "Karl wanted me to give you this," she said. "Of course I'd have dropped it in the mail if you hadn't come today, but I'm glad you did, both of you. And Karl would be pleased, too."

"We couldn't be anywhere else today," I said. "Karl made our lives possible, really."

Bruce K Beck

"Karl was the kindest man I ever met," Gabriel said. "And one of the funniest."

Emma sat Gabriel and me down and brought us a glass of wine. And I opened the letter:

Dear Kit,

I'm addressing this letter just to you. Gabriel knows already how much I love him and how much I admire his talent. And we've left nothing unsaid, really, you and I, have we? But I wanted you to know that I've already arranged to have the portrait crated and shipped to Claysville. You'll have it shortly after you read this, no doubt.

And I wanted you to know that I'm leaving the Bank Street building to Javier. No one deserves it more than you and Gabriel, but then, you don't need it. And he does. And really, what else is there? I want you two to live in that apartment just as long as it brings you joy. And I want you to negotiate a new lease with Javier that brings him a very generous return. I don't need to tell you how to do the right thing, and yet, of course, I have to say it.

My friendship with you and Gabriel has been the most precious part of my life these last decades. I've watched you both grow and blossom into extraordinary, talented men. And I've felt a delicious sense of accomplishment in having aided your journey, here and there. I might have slipped into quiet resignation had you two not shown up on my doorstep in 1972 and tugged at my heartstrings.

I've always hated good-byes. This one is perhaps the most painful. But in my role as your Fairy Godfather, I intend to continue a lively interest in your well-being. I'll be whispering in your ear and clocking your laps in the pool. When you're ordering dinner, I'll be the voice that says, "Don't forget the vegetables." And when you have board meetings, I'll be the annoying sunbeam that glints off the table and strikes your eye and makes you wonder if the choices are correct. I'll be around. How could I not?

Yours,
Karl

Chapter Twenty

The years at the Center have been richly satisfying. We never gave up Bank Street, of course. It will always be our home. But we do spend more and more time in Claysville. It took years—ten years—for Gabriel to accept the notion, but he did give up his studio in Tribeca for a new one at the Center. I had already talked to the architect who designed his gallery. He assured me he could add on studio space that would be just as open and filled with light, and that could be just as private—or not—as Gabriel wanted it to be. I said to Gabriel, "Angel, the Center needs an artist-in-residence. And you need to be the one. It's what you were born for," I said, pulling out all the stops. He knew I was working him, of course, but he also knew it was the right thing to do.

Many of the original staff are still with us. Gabriel's sister Melinda gave us a dozen years of remarkable wisdom before she decided to move on. She and her husband, Dalton, both had great job offers in Boston. So of course we had to wish them well and send them off with open hearts. It was difficult. Our little family became so close after so many years of being far-flung. But Melinda and Dalton visit now and then, and Gabriel and I get up to Boston to see them about once a year. We like

Boston, and it's always good to see what's happening at Fine Arts and the Gardner Museum.

The Prescott Center is not as important as those two institutions, of course, but we command respect around the country. And that's partly because Melinda saw to it that we launched on a solid financial footing. And because of that, we've met our goals all through the years. I think I can safely say we've given substantial, successful efforts to every education program, every community outreach project, every plan for building the collection and building attendance to see it. And we've done it in a sustainable way.

Gabriel's brother Aaron is still the Artistic Director. He gets better at the job every year, I think. It just turned out to be a perfect fit for him—and for us. And with his help we've crafted yet another ten-year plan, with extensive notes for the next one. It's all about continuity. We have to get every day right, but every tomorrow is just as important. I sleep easily, nearly every night, knowing the Center will perpetuate itself.

📖

Little Daniel Jenkins was all grown up the next time I saw him. He was working in Esther's kitchen the year Daddy died, and then he got some jobs in town. But soon Daniel headed to work in restaurants in New Orleans. He had lived there about ten years, I think, when he was on a trip home to see his family and stopped by the Center one afternoon. I took him to see Esther's grave. We were both moved by the memories of Esther and all she taught us. No,

Daniel wasn't a little boy anymore. He had become a confident—and handsome—young man. I said to him, "Daniel, would you take a look at the Culinary Center?"

"Of course," he said.

"It's named for Esther. How could it not be? I'm proud of what we started, but not so sure we've done all we can." I took Daniel on a tour of the classrooms and kitchens. He said he was impressed by the space and the kitchen equipment and by the fact that we had included all the latest technology: some video screens and projectors, and a computer database that could be expanded as needed. There wasn't all that much in those days—nothing compared to what's available now—but it looked good to a working kitchen professional.

I explained our mission the best I could: "Here's what we need to do: We need to provide top-quality training for people who want to go into the restaurant industry. Teenagers, adults, whoever. We need to provide lunches for school kids on summer break. We need to train young parents in good nutrition, and help them get tasty meals on the table. We've talked for years about lunches for seniors, but we never managed to make that a reality. I still think it's a good idea. And we need to produce the most elegant food and service in town when we're functioning as an event space." I didn't want to leave anything out of that equation. Daniel seemed to get it, that I was courting him. And then I moved in for the kill: "Would you consider directing the program?"

"I'd do anything for Esther," he said.

"But it has to be right for *you*. New Orleans is a wonderful city. Could you really come back to Claysville?"

"Could I think about it?" Daniel asked.

"Of course," I said. "I'll give you twenty minutes."

"You play rough," he said as he flashed his charming smile.

"I have experience in pursuing the right man. Nothing timid will do," I said.

"As much as I love to cook," Daniel said, "I've been thinking lately that I want something more; something that touches people's lives beyond their palates. I never dreamed it would be in Claysville."

"Tell me."

"But, yes, I think I'm ready for the challenge. And if you think I'm right for it, then yes, I'll do it," he said.

"Good," I said. "That's all I need to know. The rest will fall into place." And it did.

In the summer of 2011, Gabriel said to me, "Now that New York State has marriage equality, I think we should get married. What do you think?" I didn't know quite what to think, really. As much as equality is always a worthy goal, the idea of being legally married to Gabriel was a concept I had never dared to expect. And while I had always thought of us as married, having a license is another situation entirely. I started to think—maybe for the first time—about inheritance and the other legal complications that entered our lives with Daddy's estate and the Center, in the last decades.

We spoke to our attorney about it, and she said, "You have separate issues to deal with: As long as you keep your legal residence here, New York State will support your right to marriage and to pass-through spousal inheritance. Federally, who knows when or if? But with everything you have going on in Claysville, I think you need to be concerned about North Carolina law, too. I'm guessing they will be compelled to recognize out-of-state marriages whether they conform to state practices or not. Again, that's a guess. And again, the Federal side of it seems up in the air, too. That said, my best legal advice is that marriage will give you the best legal protections available today. Along with some of the legal instruments we already have in place."

When we got home from the lawyer's, I told Gabriel I expected a proposal. He dropped to one knee without hesitation and said, "Kit Prescott, will you marry me?" I waited a moment, for drama's sake, and then gave him an enthusiastic yes. The world felt a bit different, already—even before we tied the knot. We had dinner that evening with Jerry and Rick and asked them to stand up for us. They accepted, to our great joy. And they also confided that they were making plans, too!

Jerry asked, "Have you thought about who you want to perform the ceremony?" We hadn't, of course. Jerry said, "I know a lesbian rabbi who does marriages all the time, for all faiths—and lack thereof. Why don't you talk to her?" It seemed a good idea, so we did contact her. And she agreed to take us on. And so that's how we came to rent a party space in a favorite restaurant of ours and to say our vows before Rabbi Rachel Schwartz and a

Bruce K Beck

dozen of our best friends on a lovely September afternoon exactly forty-one years after the day we met.

The most moving part of the ceremony—for both
of us—was when Rachel read from the Song of
Songs. I didn't expect to be moved by scripture. Neither did Gabriel, and yet we both got a bit weepy:

> The voice of my beloved! Behold, he cometh
> leaping upon the mountains, skipping upon the
> hills. My beloved is like a gazelle or a young
> stag.

> My beloved spake, and said unto me, Rise up,
> my love, my fair one, and come away.

> For, lo, the winter is past, the rain is over and
> gone; the flowers appear on the earth; the time
> of the singing of birds is come, and the voice of
> the turtledove is heard in our land;

> The fig tree putteth forth her figs, and the vines
> with the tender grape give a good smell. Arise,
> my love, my fair one, and come away.

It felt good to be able to say, "I, Christopher Prescott, take you, Gabriel Williamson, to be my lawful
wedded husband." We thought about the language
in advance, of course. Both of us assumed we would
be taking a *spouse.* New York State law requires no
particular wording—just a declaration of intent. It
was Rachel who reminded us that in the act of marriage we would each of us *become* a husband and
take a husband. Gabriel and I recognized the responsibility and the honor of our new roles. We

embraced *husband.* And when we had completed our vows, then we all ate too much and drank lots of champagne. It was a glorious day.

I couldn't bring myself to send the Sargent to Claysville. We still have it. It's still hanging in the apartment on Bank Street. It's still the first thing we see every morning and the last thing we see every night when we're in New York. I realized the Sargent doesn't make any particular sense as a part of the permanent collection at the Center. It isn't regional. It isn't logical. I spoke to Jacques de Belmonte a few years ago—just before his retirement—and suggested perhaps the Met might want to purchase it from my estate. He was eager to accept my offer. And I feel, somehow, that visitors to the Met will get to savor it, one day, while visitors to the Center will benefit from the addition to our endowment.

When Momma died, we buried her in the town cemetery next to Daddy, of course. The Prescotts and the Bullards had been buried there for generations. It's how they did things. It seemed that half the town showed up for her funeral. She'd have been pleased, I'm sure. I hoped it meant we were doing something right, at the Center. Sometimes it's difficult to know. Signs—whether positive or negative—are always helpful.

What about plans—final resting places—for Gabriel and me? No plots at Pine Hill for us. Just recently I asked Gabriel to design us matching urns. I think I've found the right niche for them. And at some point, I'll have the proper little plaques made, maybe on chains to go around the necks of the urns, like the labels on whiskey decanters. "Christopher B. Prescott, Founder" and "Gabriel E. Williamson, Artist-in-Residence." And that will be our legacy. Meanwhile? Full steam ahead.

The End

This is a first edition from
Audacity Books
Please visit us on the web at
www.audacitybooks.com
For information, please send your request to
info@audacitybooks.com.

THIS IS GOD'S COUNTRY is Volume I of Bruce K Beck's **Tolerance Trilogy.** Volumes II and III will follow soon. Look for the **Love Trilogy:** Volume I, **YOU'RE SURE TO FALL IN LOVE**, is set in Provincetown, MA, in the summer of 1976. **LOVE AND THE EPIDEMIC**, set in New York City in 1986, is Volume II. Volume III, **AND LOVE ENDURES**, is set in the early 1990s. For updates, and for occasional gifts and offers, please subscribe at:

www.audacitybooks.com.

Many thanks to Sonya Teclai, Social Media Director at Audacity Books, for her support throughout the project. Particular thanks to Walter Maas for his generous wisdom. And to Richard Kutner for his classy edits. Tim Barber of Dissect Designs (www.dissectdesigns.com) signed on as a cover designer and became a friend. You're sure to fall in love, indeed. This journey would not have been possible without the example and the teaching of Joanna Penn at www.thecreativepenn.com. I am delighted, Joanna, to add this volume to your long list of books you have enabled. No doubt you will hit your one million mark any day now!

Readers are invited to listen to the
YOU'RE SURE TO FALL IN LOVE Playlist at
www.youresuretofallinlove.com

Bruce K Beck is both a writer and an accomplished chef. His novels, including the **Love Trilogy**; are available online and wherever books are sold. Before turning to fiction, Beck authored ***PRODUCE: A FRUIT AND VEGETA-BLE LOVERS' GUIDE***, which was called "gorgeous" by ***The New York Times***, "a dazzler" by ***Bon Appetit***, and "the most spectacular food book of the year" by ***The Boston Globe***. His next book was ***THE OFFICIAL FULTON FISH MARKET COOKBOOK***, which was called "invaluable" by Jacques Pépin, and "a treasure" by Irene Sax of ***Newsday***. And Rex Reed said, ". . . you'll love this book. It's like a movie!"